THE NO HELLOS DIET

a novel

ALSO BY SAM PINK

THE NO HELLOS DIET

Sam Pink

Lazy Fascist Press
Portland, OR

LAZY FASCIST PRESS
AN IMPRINT OF ERASERHEAD PRESS
205 NE BRYANT STREET
PORTLAND, OR 97211

WWW.LAZYFASCIST.COM

ISBN: 1-936383-76-4

Printed in the USA.

AUGUST 2010

It's the end of summer in Uptown, Chicago.

You start working in the stockroom of a major department store.

The store hasn't opened to the public yet.

When you go for orientation, there's already a bullethole in the front window.

As you walk into the store, a manager and a custodian stand there looking at the bullethole.

The manager says, "Just—that can't be there for too long."

The store is one of only fourteen stores—out of 2000 in the country—to be labeled "Ultra-high risk."

That's what the security guard tells you in the office area, while you wait with a group of people for your appointment time.

"Yeah man," he says, talking to you (the only one looking at him), "Since we're right by fucking Blood Alley, we'll get all kinds of assholes in here. Fucking Uptown. Just wait."

Blood Alley is two blocks of alley in the area.

Where there are prostitutes, drugs, and violence.

You nod at the security guard.

Need to get some sex and drugs and a little violence too—you think, considering you can't tell which order would be best.

Considering that almost every time period in your life looks really appealing a certain amount of time after it passes.

The security guard tells you that when the store was being built, the corporate headquarters sent down Human Resources representatives from Minnesota, and they parked their car in Blood Alley.

When they got out, a homeless guy walked up and said, "Welcome to Blood Alley" and then took his dick out of his pants and shook it at them.

"How did he shake it," you say.

Someone else says, "Yeah like up and down, side to side, what."

"Just waving his dick," the security guard says, making a motion with his hand. He smiles. "The corporate employees fucking ran down the alley screaming and shit, be all scared." He looks downward, touching his earpiece, "Ok. Yeah." Then he looks up and says, "You all can go in now."

You follow the group in, looking at the gun on the security guard's belt.

Everyone sits around a conference table while a Human Resources employee talks.

You immediately have the urge to raise your hand and say, "Yeah when's this going to be over I don't want to be here."

The Human Resources employee puts on a stockroom safety video then leaves the room.

In the video, past employees talk about safety.

They sit under dim lighting and describe how they got injured, and how they could have avoided it.

You sit quietly and listen, more and more unsure if you're hearing scary music in the video.

You consider asking the woman next to you if she hears scary music.

Then reconsider.

Whatever she answers, it will be weird.

What will you say: "Oh ok, so I wasn't just imagining that scary music, thanks" and then nod and turn back around.

In the video, this one employee talks about how she stood on a lower shelf and went to reach for something on a higher shelf, and then her wedding ring caught on the higher shelf and she fell off the lower shelf and it ripped her finger off.

She says, "I just thought I could get up and get it real quick. Just, real quick get up there and get it. Oh, but I learned. Never stand on the bottom shelf."

She tells the story with her hands in her lap and then when she gets to the part where her finger rips off, she holds up the hand and shows what remains of her finger.

Looks like a baby carrot—you think.

You consider asking the woman next to you if she thinks it looks like a baby carrot.

Then reconsider.

Across the table, an effeminate man with a ponytail and large hoop earrings says, "Oh hell no, look at that thing. Jesus Mary and Joseph."

When he notices you're looking at him, you both smile.

The employee supervising the orientation comes back into the room.

She's carrying a box of fruitsnacks and a package of juice boxes.

The tops of her breasts shake over the package of juice boxes.

Hot diggity—you think, unsure if it's for the shaking breasts or the juice boxes.

Either way.

"Ok everybody, here you go," she says in a whisper, passing around fruitsnacks and juice boxes.

Everyone says thanks, passing things to each other.

You're sweating.

You want summer to be over.

It's almost over.

It'll never be over.

You eat fruitsnacks, thinking—I'm going to bring my hammer to Chicago.

Unsure of what it means.

In the video, another person talks about how he was attaching a bungee cord to something and it snapped back and hooked his eye out, shattering the bone around the eye too.

He says, "So, I go to hook up the cord up there and, woosh"—slaps his hands—"Right back at me." He makes a hook with his finger and puts it near his eye. "Got right inside there."

His glass eye drifts sideways.

He's going to cry—you think. Maybe he cried right before the filming. Maybe right after. Either way, it's hard to tell. He's a good actor.

Other employees and stories follow.

Some narrated over video showing the safest way to do something.

For example: if a tv is on a high shelf, don't try to pull it off and catch it.

Instead, get a ladder.

And don't lean while high up on a ladder, or you might fall and hit the back of your head on the stockroom floor, resulting in severe braindamage, like what happened to this one guy in the video who can barely talk now.

And don't reach into the box compactor because it could rip your arms off.

Don't touch your eyes after handling an open box of detergent.

You nod, sitting at a conference table with other recent-hires.

You eat fruitsnacks and drink juice boxes together, silently aware that for as long as you all work there, you'll remember each other as being trained the same day.

Another employee tells a story about breaking his back.

You find yourself worried.

Something bad is going to happen.

You're going to get hurt.

Are you ready.

You can't possibly be ready.

You will touch your eyes after handling an open box of detergent.

You're going to get your finger ripped off or your eye messed up.

You're going to get mangled.

Mangled death.

Hot diggity, mangled death—you think, absolutely sure of what it means.

Eating another fruitsnack, you stare at the wall just past the television.

A tiredness so tired it's like being dirty.

Like dirt is floating from inside your body outwards out of the skin, up and out through the scalp.

Water is needed—you think. Sleep is needed. Sluts, guns, and drugs are needed.

The air conditioning activates in the conference room.

It calms you.

Almost cures every problem you'll ever have.

Almost makes you realize that you have no problems, or that problems are a giant lottery of people winning and losing, adding and subtracting—and that everyone should give him or herself preferential treatment when engaging with others, who do the same, creating justice.

You swallow a fruitsnack, thinking—Justice.

Someone taps your arm.

You turn around to the person behind you.

He says, "Ey. What's good, kid."

He's smiling.

He has small teeth, spaced widely in his gums, and small eyes, spaced widely on his head.

He has bad breath and so do you.

His is worse—you think. But it's close. Too close.

"I'eard they finna get a food place in here too," he says, still smiling. "F'sho."

"Shit," you whisper, smiling.

"Yeah, uh huh," he says. Then he lowers his head and raises his eyebrows. "S'good on account of can't be going to no Mack Donald's erry day now."

"Shit," you whisper, smiling.

"O-k?" he says, hitting your arm. He laughs, looking at the ground and shaking his head side to side. He puts another fruitsnack in his mouth. "Finna get some mo fruitsnacks," he says, tapping your arm to signal the conversation is over.

"Fruitsnacks," you say, like it's the same as "Goodbye."

In the video a different person is talking.

Having missed the first part of his story, you don't know what happened, but his head looks dented.

You're eating fruitsnacks and watching a video of a man with a dented head.

You're sad in a way that makes you want to be of use to others.

Like somehow happiness is selfish.

*

After orientation, you walk home.

Sweating new-sweat through the pasty old-sweat.

Across the street from your apartment there's a cemetery.

Every time you pass it, you'd like to know everything knowable about everyone buried there.

Everything from shoe size in eighth grade, to most gratifying insult ever openly stated/received, to grade point average junior year of high school, to worst Halloween experience.

You go into your apartment and lie down on the floor in your room.

Clothes, books, garbage, and drawings all over the floor.

A museum you've created.

The hard carpet smells comforting.

A cologne you've created.

Balled-up bathtowel beneath your head.

A pillow you've created.

You lie there smiling.

Considering that it comforts you.

And considering that you're a perfectly guarded person, unsure of what's being guarded.

And you have no complaints.

Sirens pass outside as you fall asleep.

The first effort at sleep only lasts for like, thirty or forty minutes.

But then!

You're able to keep continually falling back asleep consecutive times until deep into the next day, simply through sheer dedication and will.

Thinking about how fantastic it is, as it happens.

How it's like circling a planet made entirely of ocean, in a series of jumps. Sinking into mud between each jump.

"It feels so good to jump and sink," you mumble, between each effort at sleep.

Laughing and half-facedown on a crumb-covered sweaty-ass towel.

Effort after amazing effort.

In the future, a history teacher points to a map in the classroom and says, "What's known as, The Sleep Effort, took place here—in the Midwestern United States" then shows a picture of you to the class.

It's the end of summer in Uptown, Chicago.

You're happy that your life is happening the way it's happening.

Happening in days, where it's impossible not to just feel like some kind of random floating eyesight without any control.

An off-balanced float into the future of off-balanced floating.

A passenger in something un-piloted.

You find things happening a certain way and accept whatever way it will crash.

Over the last year, you've been a grocery bagger, a deli worker, a nanny, a Census Bureau employee, and now a stockroom employee at a major U.S. department store.

SEPTEMBER 2010

At work you have to wear a red shirt and khaki pants.

You scan things with a laser gun then lift them into carts.

Whatever people buy in the store, you retrieve from the stockroom and put on carts for the salesfloor employees to restock.

You're 27 and make fifty-cents more than Illinois minimum wage.

Every hour equals eight dollars and seventy-five cents.

Sometimes you imagine yourself in some unpainted room with the door locked, and every hour the door opens and a mysterious hand throws in eight dollars and seventy-five cents, and there is laughing, and you quickly gather the money off the ground and return to the corner.

At work the only two things to be done are scan and lift.

It's fun.

All you have to do to be a success is wear a red shirt, scan things, then lift them.

Another important goal is to avoid other stockroom employees shooting their laser gun in your eye.

Because it hurts to be lasered in the eye.

You're worried it's going to wake you up from this coma.

Worried you're going to love it.

Who knows.

At work, you find yourself doing what's supposed to be done.

Staring blankly ahead, communicating in the least way possible to co-workers.

They say, "What's up with your hair, is it like, wet from the shower still."

"No it's just greasy," you say.

They say, "Oh, that's gross."

"Who knows," you say.

Sweeping four stockrooms on each floor, avoiding conversations.

Barely saying enough to the other employees to constitute being an object that's different than all other objects.

Sometimes you think people are surprised when you talk.

Not because it's interesting, but because they didn't realize anyone else was in the room.

Like you appear from nowhere, holding a broom.

(It surprises you too sometimes though, admit it.)

Conversations don't happen.

The last conversation you remember having at work was just a manager saying, "Oh, I didn't even know you were here" when she was throwing out garbage, and then you made a sound to acknowledge you heard her.

But that's not a conversation.

At work, you also have to throw out garbage.

You load broken-down boxes into a compactor then crush them by pressing a button.

Crushing the boxes, you always say, "Die. Die. Die."

Sometimes audibly, sometimes not.

It feels the same either way.

The box compactor squeals, compacting.

Die. Die. Die.

"Die. Die. Die," you say, and watch the crushing.

Feels good to watch the boxes die.

Die. Die. Die.

Sometimes when the store closes you empty the box compactor and press the button when there's nothing in it.

And the crushing mechanism stops a little bit above the empty bottom then comes back up.

Lately, it is enough to consider that maybe when the compactor crushes without anything there to crush, a new universe opens horizontally with the crushed air.

And that maybe all the crushed atoms of air open horizontally into a new material plane of possibility.

And that maybe you've been absorbed by one, the same look on your face as always.

It is enough to consider that happening.

OCTOBER 2010

This afternoon, you do something called "Zoning."

Zoning is when there's no stockroom work for a little while, you go out into the store and line up products in the aisles, so the aisles look organized.

It's just you and Billy, this old alcoholic guy.

There's more crust in his eyes than usual, and you avoid him as you organize the candy aisle together.

Billy is in his sixties and prefers people call him Billy.

He's in a band that only plays music written by another musician "but"—he always says—"Only the more rock and roll type stuff."

He has a really whiny voice and doesn't do any work and there are always sores on his lips.

He drinks tallboys on his lunch break and then comes back and says purely descriptive things on the stockroom walkie talkie channel.

Like he'll say, "Eyyy, Billy here. Just walking up the escalator now, going upstairs—few more feet and I'm almost there" [static sound] "Okee, I'm upstairs now."

Or, "Eyyy, Billy here, I just found a press-on fingernail in a shopping cart. Probably just gonna throw it out, heh heh."

You'd rather not be alive than organizing this candy aisle.

Not meaning that in any dramatic way.

More like in a situation where a genie asked, you'd opt for being dead.

It's that simple—you think.

Suicidal thoughts always happen at the store.

(Not all of them involving a genie.)

*

Organizing the candy aisle with Billy, you realize suicide is not an option. Because the only way would be to try and bang your skull against the tilefloor hard enough. Only what would happen is, after one good bang you'd become disoriented and then get arrested and institutionalized. And then, with the eventual granting of a little personal freedom, you'd only be able to get the same type of job, where one day you'd be asked to organize a candy aisle.

You move a bag of chocolate peppermint candies forward, noticing yourself as a blur of white light on the bag's gloss.

Look at yourself straightening a bag of chocolate mints, you dumb fuck.

Fuck yourself.

Make the candy look nice, you toy.

"Billy, there's so much candy here," you say, smiling.

Billy says, "Eyy do people still use the phrase 'fudge-packer.'"

He's looking at you, leaning against shelves of candy, flicking a box idly.

"Yeah I think so," you say.

He says, "There's that one, and I hear a lot of people say 'Dirt road driver.'"

"Awesome man."

"Heh heh, yeah," he says. "It's cool. Waaah."

You're still confused why Billy adds "wah" sometimes.

"Dirt road driver," he says. "Heh heh."

Then he starts listing employees at the store who are gay.

A large percentage of the staff is gay, and he starts listing them, as though he's compiled important data.

"Yeah," you say.

You always say, "Yeah" or "Uh oh" to respond to shit you don't care about.

Which always causes a long silence.

Billy uses the silence to sing short songs to himself about whatever he's thinking, or whatever candy he's looking at.

Like, lining up bags of peppermint candy, he sings, "I got peppermint, peppermint—yeah yeah."

Or there's: "Who wants licorice, yeah yeah. Heh heh."

The peppermint song is your favorite but there's also a good one about how he's tired, and one about gummy bears.

More rock and roll type stuff.

Billy tells you about how he records music and puts it online and a lot of people listen to it.

You say, "Awesome. That's good, Billy."

He says, "Like a thousand people listened to it in Australia."

"That's good."

"Heh heh, pretty good," he says. "Wahh."

More silence.

The silence is my pilot—you think.

Because you're an idiot.

Billy says, "Think if I ever had any money I'd start an online store called 'stupidshit.com' and just like, sell stupid shit, like, and people would buy it too because people love stupid shit—heh heh."

"Uh oh."

"I know," he says. "Wahh. There'd just be all kinds of stupid shit, like where I used to work at the lotion store, yeah. And people would buy it from me, heh heh."

He coughs.

It's raspy.

Temple vein swollen.

Gray goatee.

"So you're saying if you had money, you'd start an internet store called 'stupidshit.com.'"

"Yeah 'zactly," he says. "Heh heh."

You move bags of candy forward and think about Billy and whatever terrible timeline brought him to earth.

Thinking about all the terrible timelines converging and how they make a shape that looks exactly like you.

'Zactly.

Billy pulls a few boxes of candy forward, licks the sores on his lips.

Billy.

He says, "Oh I fuggin love this fuggin one candy right here." Then, like he's talking to himself, he says, "Oh but I can't eat it. Yeah because my teeth are rotten to bits." He pronounces 'rotten' like 'rah-in.'

"What is it," you say.

He looks at you, confused. "Oh, I don't know, they're just like—" shrugs, "—rah-in, falling apart, y'know. Fuggin rah-in."

"No, what kind of candy are you talking about," you say. "Which one."

He turns and makes an oval shape with the forefinger and thumb on each hand. "It's like those things with the stuff in them," he says, squinting over the frames of his glasses. "They had the one mascot that was a tiger I think. Or a bumblebee, I'on't know."

"Oh. Awesome."

"Heh heh, yeah 'zactly," he says, going back to organizing.

"But you're saying you can't eat them because your teeth are rotten to bits."

"Yeah 'zactly," he says. "They're fuggin rah-in."

"Now as I heard it, you said they've rotted so bad they've become bits, or something of that sort."

"Rah-in and falling out, 'zactly, heh heh. Wah."

Billy tells you a story about drinking too much and falling into a kiddy pool in someone's backyard.

You say, "Uh oh."

He laughs.

Arranging bags and boxes of candy.

Why does there need to be this much candy—you think.

You're confused.

But you arrange the candy.

Not to help the store, but to make sure people know you've been there.

Billy says, "Heh heh." Then, in a Russian(?) accent, he says, "Give me dat microfilm."

You don't respond in any way except looking at the cuts on your hands, and the gray dust on your palms from tying wire around crushed boxes earlier.

(Wrapping up the wire always leaves metallic dust. You call it "gorilla hands.")

"Give me dat microfilm," Billy says again.

He's laughing in a whiny rasp, looking at you over the tops of his glasses.

You say, "Are you asking me something. I mean."

He clears his throat. "No, that's what every Russian character in every old American spy movie used to say," he says, smiling. "Give me dat microfilm. Heh heh."

He's holding back a little on the laughing.

The sores on his lips hurt—you think. Or he's trying to hide his teeth. Oh, Billy.

If you were Jesus, you'd heal his sores with a kiss and make him teeth from your bones.

No, you'd nail him to a cross with balled fists for hammers.

"Give me dah microfilm," Billy says loudly. "Heh heh, that's what they always said."

"Microfilm."

"Heh heh, yeah," he says. He moves packages of gum with one hand, raising a fist with the other. "Giff me duh microfilm."

You say, "Billy, you're just too much fun."

And there you are, the blur of white light on the bag's gloss.

You silently say hello, and move the candy closer.

"Heh heh—dat microfilm," Billy yells, shaking his fist. "Heh heh."

Organizing the candy aisle, you say, "Give me dat microfilm" over and over to each other.

Maintaining a conversation by saying the same thing over and over at varying intervals.

The same thing.

Over and over.

Laughing each time.

He says it.

Then you do.

Then there's laughing.

The fucking candy aisle.

"Give me dat microfilm," he says loudly. He curls all the fingers on one hand and holds it out at a child passerby. "Microfilm!" Then—immediately back to normal—he says, "Oh man, so I got here fuggin 43 minutes late today. S'a bummer, man. I have to walk fuggin five miles to get here and five miles back. Plus my shoes suck big time ass. Wahh. How many people do y'think are in Australia anyway."

"Sing the peppermint song again, man," you say, looking at the sores on his lips.

He laughs.

"Heh heh, I don't remember it," he says.

Billy.

Sometimes, you imagine him as a newborn baby lying awake in a crib and looking out at the night.

"Billy, this candy aisle is going to look so nice when we're done," you say.

"Yeah," he says. "Should be good."

You move a bag of candy closer.

Noticing yourself as a blur of white light on the bag's gloss.

Realizing that work is fun because at least it's a reason to leave the apartment and see people.

*

Like there's this old man who comes to the store every couple days to play the videogame displays upstairs.

He's a regular.

He comes in and stands by the videogame station and puts his face an inch from the television screen and plays without blinking.

Frozen bulldog frown—you think, watching him through the stockroom door window, right before lunch today.

He stands there in his purple sweatpants and black Velcro shoes and stares at whatever car racing game he's playing.

By his black Velcro shoes, he keeps the plastic shopping bag he always has with him.

And he drives his racecar all over the road and into other cars.

Comatose and depressing.

Maybe though, you're just dramatizing it.

Maybe coming into the store to play videogames is a fun thing he does.

Maybe he feels fulfilled while playing car racing videogames.

Maybe he races around happy and proud, and then an asshole like you comes along and feels bad for him.

You're the worst.

Depressed about another person.

That's stupid.

Yesterday after work you saw him at the bus stop in front of your apartment building.

He was holding his plastic grocery bag, and wearing purple sweatpants and black Velcro shoes.

He had on a sweatshirt many sizes too big for him and it was neon-orange with an exaggerated drawing of a big-muscled shark wearing sunglasses—the phrase "Rip It" written in "ripped-lettering" above the cartoon shark.

You wanted to walk up to him, and nod once upward with no emotion on your face, saying, "Rip it" in a quiet but assertive tone, subtly shaking your fist a few inches from your body. "Rip it, man."

Because he's a person who usually rips it, but sometimes forgets, like anyone else.

And like anyone else, you want the world to know you're a person without any intentions of ever doing anything other than just ripping it.

Just fucking rip it nonstop.

*

You pass your mandatory thirty-minute unpaid lunchbreak in the breakroom looking at the same newspaper page without reading anything.

Because you don't know where else to look.

Because there's nowhere else to look.

*

After lunch, your boss tells you to unload a palette of backpacks.

They're "Princess Gear" backpacks.

On the front of the backpack it says, "Princess Gear" in pink and purple camouflage lettering.

You've stocked it many times.

You've developed many pleasing memories, stocking it.

You've yelled out, "Princess Gear" while lasering the barcode, and then a co-worker yelled it back from across the stockroom.

You've imagined the owner of the company who manufactured the backpack, and s/he is on the phone yelling, "Look here, I need fifty thousand more goddamned Princess Gear backpacks by tomorrow goddamnit buddy, come on!"

You've taken a Princess Gear backpack out of its plastic to examine it.

It has many convenient compartments.

A place for almost anything.

You've decided it would be a good way to carry your gear if you were a princess.

You've seen yourself in a pink dress and you're reviewing what's packed in the backpack, "Wand, jewelry, snacks, butterfly knife, socks, ok."

Holding the backpack and the laser gun today, you entertain a long idea about the person who will maybe eventually own this very backpack, and how ultimately, even remotely considering a day, an hour or whatever of that other person's life—to have an experience of it as it is—would be impossible to endure. And in the terrible vertigo felt at observing even the smallest portion of any other life, there would be a death beyond anything previously experienced— happening so many times and so many different directions, that it doesn't even matter where you try to begin understanding anything, because it kills.

21

Long transitions of thought that return to certain points, in and out of people.

A passing.

With no entrance or exit.

It makes you want to die.

No, but in a good way.

You achieve a small understanding of another person, and it makes you almost die—to think through a different person, realizing something at the point where you're again resumed as yourself, standing there holding a backpack and a scanning laser.

The walkie talkie on your equipment belt comes on and someone says, "Hey, anyone know if we carry replacement beans for a beanbag chair. Not the actual beanbag, but just the beans that go inside."

NOVEMBER 2010

Your ex girlfriend still comes over sometimes.

She used to live with you but moved out and now still pays half the rent until May.

You separated when you asked her to help you carry out a garbage bag and she said no because it wasn't hers and then there were no more words.

You both just stopped talking for a few months.

You looked at each other and she left and closed the door.

And you took the garbage out the side door.

There was no hate.

Just an unspoken mutual agreement not to talk again for a while.

Came back inside the apartment and felt exactly the same.

Watching some ants that were in the garbage crawl beneath the refrigerator.

A few days later she moved all her things out while you were at work.

She left her tv with built-in vhs player in your room.

That's pretty much all there is in the apartment now except for your garbage and possibly a football somewhere.

You're not sure about the football.

Tonight when she comes by, you lie on the floor in your room and watch a videotape that was left in the vhs player. It's some show she taped off television when it was originally on.

"I'm more interested in the commercials," she says. "It's weird to see commercials you forgot about."

"Yeah," you say. "It reminds me that I hate my country. And that I won't stop until I've killed everyone in it."

She says, "Do you mind if I make a small peanut butter sandwich."

"No, go ahead."

"Do you have bread though," she says.

23

"I don't think so."

She gets up and scratches the underside of her breasts with her thumbnails.

Her t-shirt has a black and white picture on the back, a picture of the woman Ed Gein hung upside down and disemboweled in his barn.

You can almost hear the sound of the breasts gently swinging against the air as she scratches.

The gentle swing.

Yes, swing on—you think. Swing free, but come back to me. Pass over me like a carwash of breasts, swinging free against me.

After the garbage thing, she moved back in with her dad, just outside the city.

They live in Riverside, a Chicago suburb.

You lived with them a few years ago when you had nowhere else to live, before moving to Uptown.

The dad worked construction.

He had his own company.

He had a lot of money and built his own house too and it was big.

Sometimes he'd give you work.

You'd go out early in the morning and spend all day at an old house in town and break it apart, sometimes painting, or blacktopping, or whatever else.

After work he'd come home and watch simulated basketball matches on a videogame console attached to a big television.

He'd never play the videogame, just watch.

He'd set up tournaments to watch.

"Oh shit, swish," he'd say, holding the videogame controller and hitting a button to show the replay.

You'd say, "I didn't see it, what happened. Who's winning."

You and the dad never really got along.

One time, you and your ex girlfriend had an argument and she tried to kill herself with a razor and you grabbed her arms and took the razor away from her after she made a few cuts and later her dad threatened to kill you after he heard her crying and wouldn't listen to why.

One night you got really drunk and woke up in the middle of the night, openly pissing on a couch upstairs.

Woke to your girlfriend behind you, saying, "Are you fucking pissing on the couch."

You find yourself remembering all this with the understanding that the sound of her scratching her breasts is the sound of the thoughts rowing past.

24

She leaves the room.

On the videotape, there's a commercial about something that gets rid of sinus germs.

The germs are personified blob-things living inside someone's sinuses.

One of the germs walks into its germ house, takes off its outdated stereotypical hat and coat and yells, "Come on in, everybody!"—then the germ's whole family comes in and crowds the sinuses, partying.

And even though the commercial is trying to make you hate the germs, it's confusing.

Because you understand that the germs just want to live.

No one really seems at fault.

It's like, what are you then, the germ inside this apartment's sinuses.

Are you to blame too.

It's confusing.

Your ex girlfriend returns, eating a peanut butter sandwich on a single endpiece of stale wheatbread folded in half.

Where did she find bread—you think.

She says, "Hey, so guess what, it's almost sss—ahhhhk—" she chokes on the dry peanut butter and makes a cartoonish face with her eyes open wide. "Fuck," she says, pulling at the skin on her neck. "Holy shit." She swallows intensely a few times and then looks relieved. "Holy shit."

"Holy shit," you say. "Can I rub my dick on your chest for a little bit."

She lies down next to you.

Her cold feet touch your legs.

It startles you.

She says, "No I want to jerk you off and watch it go on me."

She looks at the sandwich and licks an edge a little to smooth out the excess peanut butter.

"Your breath smells bad," you say.

"Yours does too."

"Thanks for telling me," you say. "I'm going to do my best to fix it now that I know."

"You're welcome."

"You know on those medicine commercials where like, they show the germs as living things with voices and personalities."

"Yeah."

"It'd be insane if that was how it actually was. Like you feel your sinuses get clogged and then you hear a weird voice and people start partying inside your face and all over your body and they won't leave."

She's looking at you, chewing the sandwich. "It wouldn't be too bad," she says.

And you notice yourself as a blur of white light on her pupil.

"Actually yeah you're right because it'd just be normal," you say.

There's one bite of the sandwich left when she offers it.

She holds out the last bite and raises her eyebrows and says, "Hm?"

You take the last bite.

Thinking about how right now you're in the prime of your life in terms of arm and chesthair.

No this is your prime, overall.

Your ex girlfriend still comes over once in a while, but mostly you're alone.

Prime.

You don't have a relationship.

Prime.

You're just people who need a small amount of company to periodically recharge from being alone.

To stay prime.

Just people who don't want to meet new people.

Prime.

Having sex to remind yourselves you're young and capable.

To stay prime.

That's pretty much all there is.

Recharging.

More and more though, you're getting used to not needing any recharge.

Slowly reversing that need.

Viewing yourself selfishly, as something that needs no help.

Priming yourself.

*

Next morning you wake up to a lot of crust and fluid in your left ear.

You've had an ear infection on and off for the last month after getting water in your ear while showering.

And for the last week or two, brown fluid leaks out at night.

And you use twisted-up toilet paper to absorb the brown fluid.

Smells a little bit bad, like a burnt match.

And the color is getting redder.

The company you work for won't provide health insurance until you've worked there a certain amount of hours, which won't be until the end of summer, because of how they cut your hours sometimes.

So this morning, when you trade spots in the shower with your ex girlfriend, you borrow her phone and call a clinic to find out what can be done.

You have a towel wrapped around your head to dry your hair without it dripping into your ears.

You're eating string cheese.

The secretary asks a lot of questions.

You answer them.

Then you say, "I'm eating string cheese right now. Do you need to know that."

She says no.

You say, "I have a towel wrapped around my head like a girl. Do you need to know that."

She says no.

"But it's kind of fun to imagine right," you say.

She says yes.

After hanging up, you immediately miss her.

DECEMBER 2010

This morning you're awake a few hours before work.

You decide to go downtown to The Loop.

The Loop is the most downtown area of Chicago, where the subway trains all converge and make a loop at a few stops and then go out different directions.

In The Loop there are stores, offices, some universities, television/radio stations, museums, libraries, expensive condos, businesses and people.

You leave your apartment, walk towards the Brown Line train.

You stop at the 7-11 down the block.

You walk around the store and eventually grab a stick of taffy and bring it to the register.

The guy at the register is very old.

He has red eyes and big crooked teeth.

He gestures at the taffy, and in a tone of true disappointment, he says, "Dude—Vy you not get 'Mega Stick'—is two times size, and only tutty-tree cents more, man. Come on, man. Is simple."

He points at where the 'Mega Stick' size taffy is, in front of the register.

It's a neon-colored package with a small monster—eyes coming out of its skull—looking at the words "MEGA STICK" printed across the front.

You say, "Oh, shit man, thanks"—like he's just stopped you from accidentally eating a razor. "Thanks. I'll go with the Mega Stick then."

You pay for the taffy, staring at the counter.

Remember, never eat a razor—you think.

The man at the register looks at your coat as he hands you the receipt.

"Shit's reversible," you say, showing him the inside pattern. "I bought it at a garage-sale like, fifteen years ago. It was only six dollars.

Six dollars, that's unbelievable isn't it. That's like, three dollars per coat, times however many years, so it's like a dime a year I spend on having a coat."

He nods, looking at your coat. "Is a nice," he says. Then presses some buttons on the register and coughs into his hand. He refocuses his watery eyes on you. "Dude, is a icy out."

"Some blocks, yeah."

He says, "I saw a man, vuz broke his arm." He grabs one arm with the other and makes a face.

"Man," you say.

Man, I like this guy—you think.

"Ok—tenk you, sir," he says, sniffing once then wiping his wrist across his nose.

He looks to his side and starts yelling in a different language, at someone who's behind the door of the employee area.

You leave the 7-11 and walk towards the Brown Line train at Montrose.

It's cold.

The cold smells like exhaust fumes.

You're exhausted.

You walk.

Pass hair-braiding places, African restaurants, a taqueria, a gay bar, a car place, a high school with murals on the outside, and a large group of backpacked kids running.

Uptown.

Pass a store that sells t-shirts with airbrushings of cars/pit-bulls/dice/eightballs/grim reapers/naked women on them.

A tattoo shop, a liquor store, and another hair place—this one with a wall of Styrofoam heads looking out at the street.

Immigration lawyers, dentists, currency exchanges and liquor stores.

Pass them all.

You find yourself already happening.

Unfocused.

Every person you pass is a person unknown.

And you're one of the unknown people they're passing, eating taffy and staring.

This is happening.

Pass Blood Alley.

Pass another 7-11 on the next block.

A post office.

A billboard with a person in a judge costume.

Spraypaint.

Franchise sandwich places.

Other people and places.

A Hispanic guy selling tamales out of an insulated lunch box.

A blind homeless man outside the bank.

Other places and things.

Passing.

That's all.

Thinking without focus.

Why does the time before work always feel sad.

No.

You're not sure it actually feels sad.

You don't care.

You chew your taffy, feeling sick.

Worrying about how one of these bites, the taffy is going to rip all your teeth out.

How you'll just stand there holding a drooping piece of taffy studded with teeth, mumbling "Uh uh uh."

Mouth open.

Looking down at your mouth as it fills.

Trying not to swallow.

You think about how the worst thing of all would be the cold air touching the bleeding gums as you tried not to swallow.

Yeah, that would be the worst part.

At the Brown Line turnstile there's a man with no front teeth, wearing a beret and a jeanjacket.

He puts his arm on your shoulder and tries to sell you a train pass for fifty cents.

He says, "Hey, my man. Co-*mo* estas today my man, hah hah."

You look directly at him.

Feeling the closeness of your faces.

Noticing yourself as a vague shape in the whites of his eyes, which are yellow.

He backs off, takes half a plastic-tipped cigar out from behind his ear.

He holds the half-burnt cigar like a syringe, and waves the train pass at you.

"Fifty cents, fifty cents my man," he says, blinking a lot.

"No thanks," you say. "I'll trade you mine though. Mine has more money on it and you can sell it for more. You can safely stack two bills for this swollen puppy."

You think about whether or not what you just said makes sense.

The thing about the "swollen puppy."

"Fifty cents man, come on," he says. "I need to see my gramma. She hurt. She sick. Please."

You take out a twenty dollar bill from your coat pocket and give it to him.

He shakes your hand.

You get on the Brown Line to The Loop.

*

Get off at State Street.

State Street runs through downtown.

During the day it's always busy.

There's a shopping area on State and Jackson where different high school orchestras play in the winter.

Sometimes you go there to listen.

You go there and buy a drink at the fastfood lobby and sit at a table overlooking the first floor, where the orchestras play.

If there's no orchestra that day, you still stay, and make drawings on napkins or think about suicide.

Sitting in the lobby with all the homeless people.

Looking at free newspapers.

Waiting for the lake you live by to jump up and drown the city.

This afternoon there's a very tall Christmas tree, decorated in all gold.

Gold light, gold tinsel.

There are presents underneath it, wrapped in gold wrapping paper.

Next to the tree is a high school band playing Christmas music.

You sit on the second floor and watch, holding a fountain drink.

People are everywhere and moving, Christmas shopping.

How much is happening right now.

A lot is happening right now.

Don't think about it.

Sit there uncomfortable, trying to block the thought.

A million times a bajillion.

Someone walks by on a cell phone, pointing his finger downward.

He says, "But unregardless, Phillip. That's *my* can opener. And it better fucking be there when I get back."

At the table across from you, a homeless woman wearing a giant purple winterhat begins lining up plastic two-liter bottles on the table.

She has no teeth and her skin is very red.

31

Lining up her two-liter bottles on the table.

Once they're all lined up, she talks to them at random, as if in a group discussion.

She says, "Now see, the shit is so deep, it's better to find a way to swim downward and die quicker. Me, I got taught to swim downward, by my daddy. Now see, my daddy was in the C.I.A."

You sit there, watching her.

In love.

My heart is breaking—you think, for no direct reason, as you watch the woman laugh at something said by one of the plastic bottles.

And this day becomes one of the silences in between your great moments, which also appear as silences.

Passing.

You reach into your coat pocket.

Take out your ex girlfriend's phone.

She forgot it at the apartment after visiting the other night.

You access the list of pre-saved numbers, trying to read around the crack in the screen.

You type the message: "Tonight, we shall commence the blood feast" and send it to one of the pre-saved numbers.

Then select another number and send another message: "You motherfuckers thought you could drown me?"

From inside the noise of the shopping area, someone says, "Excuse me."

A woman approaches you, holding hands with her daughter.

The daughter has ice cream on her face and shirt.

The woman holds out a partially-eaten ice cream cone and says, "Excuse me, hi. Here, you can have this if you want." She leans towards you, holding out the ice cream cone. "My daughter isn't going to finish it. Here. Have it."

She thinks you're homeless.

"Oh, thanks a lot," you say, taking the ice cream cone.

"I wanted it," the girl says, looking up at the woman.

"It's no problem," says the woman, smiling. "Have a nice day."

"Yeah, thanks again, this is great," you say, lifting the cone in salute. "Merry Christmas."

"Merry Christmas," she says.

The girl says, "I still wanted it." Then she yells, "Ehhhhh."

You watch them walk off, woman walking crouched to say some things to the screaming girl.

Then they're both gone, into the outside.

You close your eyes and say, "Ahh" in regret of not seeing whether or not the woman and her daughter could give you a ride back to your apartment.

Fucking shit.

You open your eyes, finding yourself sitting in a shopping lobby on State Street, holding an ice cream cone.

This is happening.

You eat the ice cream cone slowly, letting it melt a little, then clearing up that melted area along the rim of the cone.

It's like strawberry flavored, but a little bit different.

You draw a skull over the president's face on an outdated newspaper, enjoying the ice cream.

Thinking thankful thoughts.

Thinking this is surely just the first of what will be many victories today.

Admitting to yourself that sometimes it's worth going outside and meeting people.

Sometimes not.

Sometimes difficult to tell.

Sometimes not.

In the middle of a shopping lobby on State Street, there's a Christmas tree decorated in gold.

And you think about yelling a yell that you don't stop until it feels like you're about to vomit from the scratching sensation in your throat and/or you pass out from exhaling.

Your shift is 4 p.m. to 11 p.m. tonight.

Not bad.

*

Take the Red Line train out of The Loop and get off at the Wilson stop, a block from where you work.

The Wilson stop has been voted the worst stop two years straight by the people who live in Chicago.

Worst of all the stops made by the eight different-colored train routes.

A news station holds a vote every year and the people voted the Wilson stop the worst, twice.

The reasons were: piss-smell, shit-smell, the homeless, and violence.

This winter will be the winter of shit, piss, and violence—you think, turning onto Broadway Ave.

In the back of a car stopped at a redlight, a small girl looks at you through the windshield.

You stare at each other as the car drives away.

Passing.

One long forward float.

You walk the last block, admitting to yourself that your life sometimes feels like a floating that's no-fun.

Looking blankly out at a future.

Going into it.

Already happening a certain way.

An off-balance float.

People are entering the store through the front entrance, and some stand around out front trying to sell magazines or just asking for money.

You go to the loading alley of the store.

The stockroom entrance.

On the side of the store facing the Red Line train-tracks, there's a big banner of the company's logo.

The banner is composed of many smaller reflective pieces, so that when the Red Line train passes nearby on the bridge structure, the banner waves.

One of your co-workers is shaking off a dust broom underneath the reflective banner.

"Hey hey. What's good, faggot," he says.

You don't say anything.

Walking up the loading ramp.

Going into the stockroom.

One day when you get to work, maybe you'll be brave enough to just keep walking.

Maybe one day, you'll just keep walking and see what happens.

Probably not though.

Either way, when you enter work today you're comforted.

Thinking about the high schoolers from the orchestra on their bus-ride home, and the lives they're living with each other.

It's comforting.

*

On your first fifteen-minute break, you're drawing on a papertowel in the breakroom.

The tv is on very loud, showing a remake of a movie about a giant gorilla.

A microwave dings behind you.

A woman named Chavon takes a plastic tray of food out of the microwave and sits down at a different table.

Half her head is braided.

The other half is puffy.

She's been calling you "Texas Ranger" ever since you shaved your beard and left the moustache.

A few days ago she asked if she could be your "black sidekick."

"What this shit, Texas," she says, nodding towards the tv.

You look at the tv.

"It's some gorilla shit," you say.

"This some crazy-ass rainforest shit?" she says. "Ey. Ey, you think I cook this wrong."

She holds up her plastic dinner tray, fingertips on the edges.

The plastic is shriveled.

"Yeah," you say. "If the plastic gets hot enough to make that happen then it's poisonous, I think. I don't really know though."

"Should be fine I bet," she says, setting the tray on the table.

She reaches for a plastic bag by her feet and unscrews the lid to a gallon of orange juice.

She drinks some of the orange juice, tv screen reflected in her glasses.

"The fuck is this shit now," she says, capping the orange juice. "You see this. Fuck is this. Damn. Look at those."

In the movie, a man wakes up surrounded by huge, toothed worm-things.

"This some nonsense, damn," Chavon says. "Fucking run! How come he ain't run yet."

You yell, "Run, idiot."

The worm-things attack the man.

Every time a worm-thing jumps at him, he punches it on top of the head, yelling, "Yah."

It happens many times in a row.

"Yah. Yah. Yah."

You and Chavon start laughing.

Off-screen, another man screams.

The camera cuts to him.

There's a huge bug on him.

It scares you.

"Oh shit," Chavon says.

You look at Chavon and say, "Fuck, that scared me."

"Hell yeah," she says. She peels off the plastic cover on her dinner.

Steam burns her. "Shit," she says, shaking her hand. "Oh what that worm do to him. I miss it?"

You say, "Fucking worm went to bite him again."

Chavon stands from her chair a little and yells, "Punch that motherfucker then!"

"Punch that motherfucker," you yell, losing enthusiasm halfway through.

More people walk into the breakroom.

Chavon leans back in her chair and says, "Hey, any you all want the macaroni and cheese in this thing. They'idn't have the one with the mashed potatoes like I like. I know it sound crazy, but I'on't like no cheese. Fucking taste bad to me. Finna give it to someone at least."

She's holding the shriveled plastic tray up in the direction of the people who have just entered the breakroom.

One person says, "Nah Chavon. Thanks though."

Another, "Yeah I don't want it, thanks."

Another, "No, thank you."

Another is a skinny guy with his hair dyed blond and black, and a piercing through the middle of his nose and a tattoo covering his entire arm.

He shrugs and says, "If nobody wants it."

Chavon hands him a paper plate with the macaroni and cheese on it.

He leans against the countertop by the sink, blowing on the plate.

Chavon says, "I'on't know what it is, but I'on't like no cheese. It be fucking irritating me."

The guy gestures to Chavon with the food in his fingers and says, "Thanks. Thank you."

"Oh, you welcome," says Chavon. "Glad somebody wanted it."

"Chavon you're so polite," you say.

During a commercial break there's a commercial about an upcoming episode of a show where people live in a house together and get drunk and then argue and fight.

Chavon leans back in her chair. "Shit," she says. She laughs, makes a clicking sound with her front teeth. "Give me a motherfucking show—I act a fool fo ya. I'on't need no script neither."

Another woman in the room laughs the word "Shit" in agreement. She has an extremely large ass and she's wearing a bronze-colored weave. "Chavon, let me buy a cigarette off you," she says. She's eating a candy bar, and switches hands to lick her thumb. "Let me get two actually." She waves at you with the hand of the thumb being licked, raising her eyebrows at the same time.

You say, "Hi Lawanda."

"Heyyyy," she says.

"How's Greg Junior," you say.

That's her son's name.

She told you a while ago.

"Did he like his birthday party," you say.

"Oh G.J.?" she says, smiling. "He fine, he fine." She's holding out a dollar bill between her first and middle finger, waiting for Chavon. "Yeah, he good," she says. "He always wanna be whining 'bout when I leave. He say"—she poses and uses a whiny voice—"'Don't go mommy, don't go.'"—then back to normal tone—"He miss his mommy that's it."

You nod and say, "Yeah."

Chavon leans back in her chair, going into her pocket. "I'on't need no script neither. Just give me the show and I act a fool. Shit. Fuck it."

Lawanda says, "Chavon, you always acting a fool anyway. Talking 'bout."

Chavon makes a clicking sound with her front teeth.

She takes out a pack of cigarettes.

She says, "I'on't need no script neither," with her eyes open wide looking at the floor.

Her and Lawanda trade money and cigarettes.

In the movie, other things are happening.

It's hard to tell what's computer-generated and what's not.

Everything seems computer-generated, including the people.

Fuck it.

You rub your eyes in a deeply satisfying way and lean back, stretching over the chair.

Your spine cracks and you yawn.

Chavon is doing the same thing.

You notice each other and laugh, mid-yawn.

Chavon claps her hands once and points.

"That feel good as hell right now don't it," she says.

"Yeah," you say, smiling. "I love stretching this way."

She laughs loudly. "Me too. Shit."

Then you stretch your arm a different way as if it's a regular stretch you do—only you've never done it, and it hurts.

You give yourself thirty more minutes for your fifteen-minute break, drawing lines across the papertowel as close and straight as can be drawn.

Each on top of the other.
It looks nice.

*

At the end of the shift you have to return your equipment keys to a security guard.

He's sitting on a stool up by the front, watching a computer display of various cameras in the store.

He's combing his hair back with a small black comb.

You don't remember his name.

You hand him the keys and smell your hand.

"Which ones are these," he says, looking at the computer screen.

"Backroom #3," you say, smiling for some reason.

You can't control it.

It overpowers you.

Involuntary smiling.

"Thanks," he says, and puts the keys in his chest pocket. "Rock on, cowboy."

You notice yourself as a blur on his badge, as he goes back to combing his hair with the small black plastic comb.

You wish you had the exact same comb, right now.

You'd take it out and make the same motion with it whenever he does, making direct eye contact.

"Hey man," he says, "This is going to sound weird, but when you're in the back there, do you ever think about your arm getting ripped off by that box smasher thing."

You look him in the eyes and nod.

"Yeah, every day," you say.

He exhales through his nose quickly. "Man I've thought about it too," he says, combing the back of his head.

He keeps the non-combing hand above the comb as he combs.

A good method—you think. A great method.

He says, "Every time I'm fucking back there, and I hear that squealing sound, I just know I'd get my arm caught in there eventually, then just have to stand there and take it." He pauses, staring. He makes a face and touches his shoulder. "Fuck man—that slow ripping."

You don't answer.

Something will happen.

Something will change what's happening.

The doors to the store open.

Customers and cold air come in.

A group of girls comes in, laughing and talking.

The security guard and you both turn and look at the same time.

He says, "Oh damn kid. I'd fuck all of them"—motioning with the tip of the black plastic comb towards the girls.

"Would if what," you say—looking at the girls, wondering if they're going to use a shopping cart or not.

"I don't know," he says, "but—" He laughs through his nose again and says, "But, shit man."

"Butt-Shit Man."

"Butt-Shit Man forever," he says, nodding.

Both his lips are bent inward.

His fat chin.

His combed-back hair.

He's beautiful.

Your life, beautiful because of him.

Admit to yourself you want his action figure.

Admit you want to play with it while taking a bath, like just hold it down under the water for a long time.

Or no you don't have a bath, so in the shower you'd hold the action figure against your dick, letting the water hit you.

The security guard puts the keys in a drawer beneath the computer.

He says, "Ha, we had to throw this guy out today because he was walking around and pinching people's asses. They were full-pinches too."

He demonstrates one on your arm without consent.

"Like that," he says.

The pinch hurts.

You make no face.

"Like that," you say.

Then, holding the pinched area, you explain to him the three or four main reasons you don't like baseball.

You say, "Alright have a nice night."

He doesn't say anything.

Which seems just-right.

Completed.

*

In the locker area, you get your coat and keys, and the apple you didn't eat at lunch.

A girl next to you is about to start the overnight shift.

She opens a locker and puts her stuff away.

"Fuck," she says, "I'd rather be anywhere than here right now. Just"—closes her eyes—"anywhere but here. Fuck this place, seriously."

She puts her phone and keys into a locker and uses chapstick on her mouth.

"What about in the middle of a forest fire," you say. "With a mouthful of burning pine needles. How about there. Just burning to death in a huge forest like that, with no one to help you."

She moves her head back and raises her eyebrows. "Shit I'd rather be sipping Kool Aid with Satan His-self in Hell, than be here right now."

"I can fit my whole coat into this small locker," you say, forcing the coat back into the locker then closing the locker for proof.

"Nice work," she says.

When other employees complain about being at work, you know they're just trying to create some common emotion.

But you also know it doesn't matter.

It's impossible to care about being at work.

Because you never have anything to do, so it's impossible to get upset about not being able to do it.

It'd be fake.

*

Back out front of your apartment, you stand by the bus stop and eat your apple.

A police SUV circles the block.

A few nights ago someone got shot in the alley behind your apartment building, so there are more police out.

You think about how police control—thought out to its conclusion—would require an infinite amount of people watching over the people watching over others who may not even be able to be watched over on account of having to watch over someone else.

You put the apple core in the metal garbagecan by the bus stop.

You ring the buzzer for your apartment, just to test if anyone is inside waiting to attack.

Inside your apartment, you look at yourself in the mirror on the back of your bathroom door.

Deciding your hair is at a "Level 6" greasiness.

Deciding that "Level 6" is characterized by not only appearing wet, but almost "oozed."

"Oozed," you say, touching your greasy hair.

You consider calling off work tomorrow.

I'm just too oozed, I can't come in, sorry.

The thought of calling off work is like the thought of suicide, just nice to think about.

"You, my friend, are a handsome man," you say, making direct eye contact with yourself in the mirror.

Feeling acutely bothered by the tag of your shirt.

Feeling like you're already happening.

JANUARY 2011

No work today.

You go to the currency exchange to cash a recent paycheck.

400 united fucking states dollars.

You're next in line.

In front of you there's a homeless woman wearing a backpack.

She's at one of the windows with an employee.

The employee keeps saying, "I need a form."

And the homeless woman wearing the backpack keeps responding with one or two short shrieks.

She keeps communicating that way to the employee, shrieking and holding her hands up.

Everyone in the currency exchange is ignoring her.

You're looking right at the back of her head.

Her voice scares you.

Then she's just saying, "uhh uhh" like a person doing an impression of a monkey.

She adjusts her backpack, walking backwards away from the window.

The currency exchange employee ignores her, waving you to come forward.

It's your turn.

You cash the check.

Feeling that something is wrong the whole time.

Like something has already gone wrong.

But that's how everything feels—you think, smiling.

Considering that maybe you're making the same shrieking sounds, even though it feels like you're talking.

Goddamnit.

That could be happening.

The currency exchange employee cashes your paycheck.

400 dollars.

You envision yourself getting robbed outside.

You envision a complex series of attacks perpetrated on you by a robber, where you gracefully defend each attempt.

Lately, you always seem to be thinking of ways to defend yourself if something happens, no matter what happens.

You think of things that could happen and then how you'd defend yourself.

But then you can't even think of what you'd want to be defending.

Outside on the corner of Montrose and Sheridan, it's cold.

Some wind blows into your infected ear and it hurts.

People are out, walking and doing whatever.

Living.

400 motherfucking dollars.

A younger woman passes you, holding the elbow of a much older woman, who keeps saying, "Muh muh muh."

You want to approach her and say, "Muh muh?" with a confused look on your face, then point at her like yes, it is indeed the person you thought it was. "Muh muh!"

On the corner of Montrose and Sheridan, things are happening.

This is happening.

This is you.

And it feels like freedom.

But it's shitty.

And you can't describe how.

400 motherfucking dollars worth of indescribable shittiness.

*

You use some of the paycheck to buy a bed.

There's a small bedding store under the Red Line tracks on Broadway Avenue.

The bedding store is next door to a chicken place that has chickens painted on the windows and the man chicken is looking at the woman chicken's legs and the caption underneath says, "Only a rooster can get a better piece."

You go into the bedding store.

Inside, you're unable to tell if it's a store or someone's apartment.

It smells like some kind of deodorant you used when younger, which saddens you, and you feel you might fall over.

A salesperson walks out from the back area and says, "Hi boddy, how are you. Hi hi."

His hands are in his pockets the whole time.

It bothers you and you don't know why.

On top of his head there are maybe twenty to thirty hairs and just as many moles and you want to name them all, then introduce them to each other.

"I'm fine," you say. "Can I see whatever bed costs the least, please."

"You want something easy on pockets, boddy," he says, scratching his chin on his shoulder.

"I want the one that costs the least."

The salesperson nods and walks you to the back area.

The bed is leaned up against the wall to the backroom.

It's very small and thin.

It's purple, with the word, "Kiddddzzzzzz" printed on it, in different areas with different colored lettering, as if exploding.

The salesperson says, "Forty dollars for this option here."

"Which option," you say.

"This option," he says. "Right here. Kids bed."

He sniffs.

Takes his hand out of his pocket, puts it on the "Kiiddzzz" bed.

At this point, you realize how awesome it'd be if he's been keeping his hands in his pockets because they were claws/insect pincers—maybe just skeletal.

"Forty dollars for this option," he says, tapping the bed.

"Is this a good option."

"Pretty good option here," he says, putting his hand back into his pocket. "Springs good. No stains. Everything good. Kids bed basically."

"And this option is easy on the pockets, you said."

"Forty dollars," he says. "Sooo good, boddy."

"A good option," you say, nodding.

"Yes yes," he says, hands in pockets.

Hiding his hands again—you think. He's reaching for something. Have to kill him. Have to finish him first.

"Forty dollars," he says. "Also, can't help you carry it, boddy. Sorry man. Back is fock-up. No debit card, k?"

"Yeah, ok."

For some reason you don't want it to be over though.

So you pretend to examine the bed.

The pretend-examination involves moving the bed a few inches off the wall and checking behind it, then pinching the fabric a little in a way that suggests examination.

This is a pretty good examination—you think.

And you realize your forehead muscles are painfully flexed.

It's hard to relax them but then it feels good.

The salesman sniffs loudly. "Really, for forty bucks, is good option, boddy," he says.

"I think I'm going to go with this forty dollar option then."

The salesperson looks comatose, staring at the bed and nodding. "Ok, you carry though, sorry guy, k?" he says again, shrugging with his hands still in his pockets.

"Ok, I understand."

You give him two twenty dollar bills then leave the store.

Snowfall has started.

It's mild.

The flakes hit the ground and reverse into nothing.

You carry the bed home, six or seven blocks under an increasing snowfall.

The bed helps to block the snow a little bit from your head and face, carrying it on your back, holding the loops on the side.

A soft shell.

Snowflakes hit your fingers and hands, but nothing else, carrying home the Kiiiddddzzz bed during a snowstorm.

This will be a good memory—you think. Can't wait to remember it.

You put the bed directly on the floor in your room.

No frame, no boxspring.

The second or third night after buying it, you wake up to the sound of two people fighting in the alley across the street.

The sound of feet scratching against ice and alley rocks.

The sound of some yelling.

Then hitting sounds.

Then someone saying, "Stop stop stop, ahh—ahh."

Then quiet.

You lie there on the "Kiiiiiiddddzzzzz" bed, listening.

People.

Places.

Things.

Kiiiiiddddzzzz.

Happy New Year.

FEBRUARY 2011

There's this other guy who works in the stockroom and everyone calls him "Sour Cream."

Because one time he got stopped by a customer in the store and when asked for the location of sour cream, he just panicked and said, "Sour cream sour cream sour cream" repeatedly into the walkie talkie.

You became friends when you were both in the breakroom one time and the news showed an old woman throwing the first pitch at a baseball training camp.

She tried to throw the ball and it looked funny and you both looked at each other while laughing.

Sour Cream wears fake diamond earrings.

His real name is Jesús.

He has three lines shaved into the hair on the side of his head, and a longer area of hair on the back of his head, like a rat tail.

Today you're unpacking boxes of underwear and t-shirts in an upstairs stockroom, and he tells you about a hat he bought off the internet, a hat that has a built-in ponytail.

"I'ma fucking rock that shit, jo," he says. "Ponytail hat. I wanted to get it expedited shipping or whatever but that shit was fit-teen dollars."

"Fuck that," you say.

"Fuck that, jo."

"It'd be funny if they sent you a blond one," you say.

"Nah son, I got the black-colored one. It'll look fucking bad-ass."

Then he starts talking to you about female co-workers, and what he would or would-not "do to them."

While he's talking about what he would do to the females in the store, you entertain yourself by thinking about running out into the store screaming, exaggerating the cords in your neck as you scream—hands at sides, all fingers curled.

46

Sour Cream says, "Hey man would you let Janisha straddle your face and shit, like backwards and shit and rub her ass all over your face."

You think about it.

The part about "letting" is confusing.

Plus 90% of the people he's mentioning aren't familiar.

You say, "I'd have to like, be in the situation to know. It's hard for me to say."

Sometimes instead of sexual things, he suggests situations with two unfortunate choices, to see which one you'd pick.

Like: "Alright man, would you rather drink piss—like, right out the dick—or, get raped in the ass with a screwdriver. I'd drink the piss."

He likes to talk about things so that he'll have a chance to give his own answers and the reasons behind the answers.

Seems to like mentioning dicks too.

Like whenever you tell him you just swept or threw out garbage or whatever, he'll say, "That's big-dick shit right there, man. We some big-dick hustlers"—and then he'll hold up his forearm and you hit forearms together.

Sour Cream has the skyline of Chicago tattooed on his forearm, with "Chicago" written beneath in cursive.

"Alright what about Charlotte, bro," he says, nodding upwards once. "Would you fuck Charlotte for a million dollars, bro."

Charlotte works the fitting rooms.

She was born a man but surgically became a woman.

That's why he's asking you.

This, like, means something to him.

He's evaluating you.

Looking for a good opportunity to call you gay/faggot/bitch/pussy.

"Charlotte, man," he says, "And you have to fuck her until you jizz an'shit."

You scan a package of underwear and put it on a shelf in the stockroom.

"I have to jizz *and* shit," you ask. "What are the terms here."

"You have to nut, jo. A million dollars though man, come on," he says. "It's crazy huh. Too gross. I don't even know. I don't even know, jo. Can't even say."

"Let me make one thing clear, man," you say. "I'm going to destroy the United States, ok. Fucking destroy it. Did you hear me. The whole thing. Every state, every person, every dog, cat, and dream. Listen to what I'm saying, now. This is important. It's time to start over from nothing."

"Ell yeah, son," he says, snapping his fingers once. He hits your arm with the back of his hand. "That's big-dick shit, son. That's some big-dick shit right there, guerro."

"The final destruction is still to come. You're either in my army or dead."

He nods upward and says, "Who the big-dick hustlers. Let's just clear this shit up right now, guerro."

"We are."

"That's it," he says.

He holds out his hand.

You slap it, move into a shake, then pull each other in for a small hug—patting each other's backs before continuing to stock packages of underwear.

The laser guns make beeping sounds through the quiet.

Every time the laser touches a barcode, the gun beeps twice.

Beep-beep.

You barely notice it anymore.

But it used to sound like mocking-laughter.

Beep-beep = Ha ha.

You used to be worried the beeps were a way for the company to implant messages in your head to control your behavior—but then realized you'd never know because that very thought could've been put in your head by the company.

Fear.

"Big-dick hustlers," Sour Cream says, filling up a shelf with packages of underwear.

You want to ask Sour Cream if he thinks there are messages in the beeps, but he might be put here to spy on you.

He could be one of them.

Nice try, you fucking spy—you think.

You think about a map of the U.S.A., a fist punching through it from behind.

Sour Cream lasers a package.

Beep-beep.

"Some big-dick shit," he says, scanning and stocking another box. "Must be big-dick shit all day today, I'on't know. S'crazy."

You shoot the laser at his eyes a few times but keep missing.

The laser crosses his face in a straight line, on and off.

"Quit it bitch," he says.

He checks messages on his phone, holding it next to the laser gun to make it seem to the security cameras like he's working.

He sings, "Big-dick hustlas—it's who we are, son—we fucking awe-some."

Then he does a dance where he holds his arms a certain way and then just bobs up and down.

Good singing voice—you think. Good dancing too.

You say, "Hey man, are you ever worried about getting bit by a spider while you're stocking bananas in the produce cooler. That could happen. Have you thought about that at all, or no. Like a spider from South America could be in the bananas and fall asleep or get paralyzed by the cool temperatures on the way to the store and then come to life and bite you and you'd die. Stocking bananas for minimum wage, you'd get bitten by a spider and fucking die. Is that what you want."

Sour Cream scans a package and stacks it.

"Damn, jo," he says. "I'm worried about it now, little bitch. That's scary as hell, man. I hate spiders. Why you think about that type of shit, El Guerro."

He starts scratching at his chest, laughing.

Laughing, but clearly worried now.

Worried about the spider.

Your plan is working.

Always be worried about the sleeping spider—you think. But how long will the spider sleep. Ah, yes.

Sour Cream scratches at his chest.

He says, "Damn son, I been eating a lot of peanut butter and shit, and it's making me get these big-ass pimples on my chest. Shit hurts. I can't pop that shit either." Then he affects an overly Caucasian voice and says, "It's excruciating. I think I just need an organic chai tea and my slippers."

You both laugh.

"Can I borrow your keys," you say. "I have to go do the garbage before lunch."

"Yeah," he says. He throws the keys. "Oh, hey man, check this out."

He presses some buttons on his phone and shows you a picture of a girl.

The girl looks really young.

She's smiling and making a face that other people have probably told her is cute.

"Had this bitch suck my dick three times last night," he says.

Looking at the picture, you say, "I'll sweep later too, I don't mind.

After I do garbage I mean."

He nods, pocketing his phone.

"That's right, babygirl," he says. "'Cause you a big-dick hustler."

"Thanks man."

You walk away, feeling self-conscious about your butt.

Earlier, Sour Cream complimented you.

He said, "No homo shit, but—you work out man? You exercise? You look nice and fit, you know" and then said other things to make sure you understood it in an objective way.

Walking to the garbage area, you hit the keys against your leg and imagine a mummy walking out from behind an aisle then coming towards Sour Cream with its arms out.

And in a dusty and decayed voice, the mummy says, "I'm gay"—and Sour Cream dies in terrified silence as he's strangled to death by the gay mummy.

*

After doing the garbage and going on lunch, you pass time in the main office staring at a list of the month's birthdays.

Shit, it's Daisy's birthday tomorrow.

Who's Daisy.

Daisy is a nice name.

You consider changing your name to Daisy.

You take the escalator upstairs and go to a remote bathroom unknown to most non-stockroom employees.

It's your secret bathroom.

Whenever you use it, you feel like you're being followed, until the overwhelming relief of getting inside and locking the door.

You get inside and just stand there breathing the fake fruit scent from the air freshener.

Today you take off all your clothes and fold them, putting them on the ground next to your feet.

Sometimes you're only able to shit if completely naked (socks and untied boots still on).

And to the tune of "This Is The Song That Never Ends" you sing, "This Is The Man With No-o Friends"—lightly picking a scab loose on your shin the whole time.

A lot of shit comes out of you.

It lands in a clay pile above the water on a mass of toilet paper someone left in the bowl.

Smells truly sickening.

You sit there, staring at the shitty water.

The walkie talkie on your equipment belt goes on.

"Eyy Billy here, just talked to a customer for a while about potting soil for a while but, um, I'm coming to the backroom now and I'm by the hygiene aisle so I'll be there up there soon. It's so hot in the store today isn't it. Jesus frickin Christ knock it off with the heater, right? Heh heh alright." The walkie talkie goes off. It comes back on. "Oh one more thing, if anyone needs a lawnmower, I'm try'n sell one. So"—he pauses—"Okee. Wahhh."

Flushing away the shit, you wonder about when you'll not be paying attention and end up dying at work—like in a machine, or falling off a ladder, or meeting a vengeful skeleton that has risen from entombment in the concrete of the stockroom floor.

*

Outside the bathroom, Sour Cream is unloading a palette of small Christmas trees onto a shelf marked "Clearance Items."

He always makes sure to follow you so he can keep talking about things you don't want to talk about.

He always finds you because he doesn't like to be alone.

If he's alone he probably just imagines dicks—you think. Dick pandemonium all around him. A rotating tower of dicks coming at him. "Get the fuck away from me, dicks!" he yells, as the shadow of the dick machine covers him.

"Alright man," he says, lifting a box and stacking it. "What about. Alright, shit. What about the girl at the front desk. Vanessa. Listen to the whole thing before you answer now, guerro. Would you, lick her asshole for a million dollars."

It seems like he's going to say more, so you wait.

He doesn't say anything else.

"Is that the whole thing," you say.

"Yeah," he says, pushing a stray Christmas tree limb back into a box. "A million for the asshole. Just like, go buffet on that shit, jo."

He's been on the 'million dollars' thing a lot.

'Buffet' too.

You say, "I'd do it for a lot less than a million. Probably even for free. Actually yeah, for free."

"Damn, jo, you'd do that?" he says. "Total asshole though. All around it, bro. Like the whole radius and shit."

He makes a gesture with both his hands like he's framing a painting or a camera shot for a movie then he puts his face by the frame and opens his mouth, tongue flipping all over.

The sound of his tongue flipping around hurts your chest in some weird way.

"Same answer, yeah," you say.

He claps and says, "Damn jo. El guerro like eating some ass? That fucking ass buffet? You do that?"

"You're saying you wouldn't do that, even if someone was going to give you a million dollars."

"What. Nah man. Hell nah."

"So you'll come here four or five times a week and make an incredibly small fraction of a million dollars, but you won't lick a cute girl's asshole for the money. That's your stance."

He makes a clicking sound with his teeth. "You fucking bogus, guerro. Entirely fucking bogus."

He hydraulically forklifts down another palette of Christmas trees.

You take turns stacking the boxes on lower shelves.

"How do you say 'octopus' in Spanish," you say. "I feel like an octopus when I'm working hard, like—" and you make a swirling motion with both your arms going around your waist.

"Pulpo," he says.

"It's like I'm El Pulpo sometimes here."

He laughs twice in a high pitch, and claps once. "El Pulpo, witcha greasy-ass mullet. You fucking sick motherfucker."

You continue stacking boxes.

Some of the boxes are open along the sides.

Staples and wire treelimbs scratch as you lift.

You say, "Tell me how sexy I am again, you little shithead. I want to hear it again from those pretty lips."

"Chill faggot," he says. "Fucking kill you." He clicks his teeth and says, "Man, hope I get out early tonight, jo. Finna fuck this one bitch that live by my gramma's place."

"Nah, you're a virgin," you say.

"Nah," he says. "Nah, big-dick style, babygirl. Thought I told you."

You're looking at his rat tail.

Not bad—you think.

"How long did it take you to grow your rat tail," you say, nodding backwards and pointing at the back of your neck.

"Like, three months, nigga," he says, holding down his pointer-finger with his thumb and spreading out the other three fingers.

His pinky nail is really long.

"What if I grow a rat tail and let it get way longer than yours," you say. "How would that make you feel."

He doesn't answer.

He checks his phone, holding a box upright with his other hand.

He needs to be demeaned by a bigger rat tail—you think. He needs to be shown his place on the rat tail foodchain. How long is the longest rat tail ever. Doesn't matter. It can be exceeded. It can be done.

Sour Cream throws a box up onto a shelf and pulls his pants up. "You all right man?" he says. "You look like, sick or some-shit. You ok? You getting skinny on me, guerrito? What's good. Don't get skinny on me now, babygirl."

"I'm good," you say. "As long we're together, I'm good."

He puts a box up on a shelf and some fake pine needles fall out of the box onto his face. "Chill faggot," he says.

You lift a box and stack it on the one he just stacked.

"Sour Cream, it's time to destroy America. Don't you think. It's time. You either help me or I kill you first."

"It's big-dick time, babygirl," he says, snapping.

"Big-dick time," you say.

"Ell yeah," he says.

And you watch him stack another box.

His rat tail shakes.

*

You pass the last ten minutes of your shift standing by the punch-out clock.

There's a girl on her cell phone, yelling at someone.

She's openly crying, walking around the locker area.

"No but that's because you an asshole," she says, looking intensely at the ground and pointing her finger down at the same time. Her hand is tattooed. "Ass, hole. Like, you the very part of the asshole where the hole touches at all points."

"Asshole," you yell, in the direction of the phone.

The girl on the phone raises her hand.

You high-five her.

*

Outside it's windy.

Your infected ear clicks and goes close to deaf while you're walking home.

At the corner of Broadway and Montrose, a sick-looking man stares at you until you stare him into not staring.

You pass a section of Blood Alley that goes behind a pizzeria.

You see a group of men in wheelchairs, gathered in the alley.

They hide small pipes in their sleeves, smoking crack.

They're from a retirement home nearby.

They're veterans.

You recognize them from Census work you did at a soup kitchen.

Maybe you should become friends with them.

They seem fun.

The only friend you have is your ex girlfriend and you don't actually like her and she doesn't actually like you.

Smoking crack in the alley with the wheelchaired men might be the needed alternative.

You've smoked crack before, three or four times.

Each time acquired for free, each time smoked alone.

Like the first time, you went with a friend to get his oil changed and a guy at the oil change place asked you for a ride home and gave you crack for driving him.

You thought it was ok.

Wasn't anything more or less than ok.

Just something that happened.

Just you high on crack cocaine in your cold bathroom, sitting fully-clothed on the toilet, staring at the exhaust fan and rubbing your face.

That's it.

Then back to life.

Which is always the exact opposite of high on crack.

Which isn't anything more or less than ok.

Just something that happens.

Maybe you need a wheelchair for crack to be fun.

Maybe you need to find out.

On the block before your apartment building, you see your ex girlfriend's car parked by a meter.

She used to smoke crack when you were in high school.

Your ex girlfriend and you transferred to the same high school from the same place, and started at the same time, as sophomores, all without knowing each other.

That's where you first met.

You were both the new people at the same time.

In high school, you went out a lot to vandalize homes.

And one night you and some other people drove to this remote subdivision. At the first house, you broke windows, some lawn furniture and then lit the trampoline on fire in the backyard.

It was a big trampoline.

You slashed the top of the trampoline with a butterfly knife then poured lighter fluid all over it and lit it on fire.

Before you even got to your friend's car—idling a block away—the fire was already too high.

You found out it was her house later on, after vandalizing it but before moving into it.

And everyone talked about how you lit the fire, but no one ever found out for sure.

The only people who knew were the people there.

And they blamed you too, to remove themselves from being there.

But nothing ever happened.

Then years after high school you saw her again, at a New Year's party.

You kissed her hand at one point, because you vowed to kiss someone's hand before you got there, and it resulted in a relationship, even though she still thought you burned down her trampoline.

You watched her cry the first few weeks, still upset about the trampoline.

But you never told her you did it.

You denied it.

Then finally one night she said, "Alright. It was just so bad because that trampoline was like the only time me and my dad would get along. It felt bad when someone took that, you know. And I thought it was you. It felt so bad. I hated you. You were cute though."

To which you silently agreed, looking at your lap and nodding—reminded of how exciting it was to be close to a fire that big.

Walking upstairs to your apartment, you know she'll be inside.

You see a very small hole in the stairs that opens into light and the first floor hallway below.

And for a second, it's genuinely thrilling.

Because it seems like the discovery of a hidden floor.

Where new people live.

People who could only be important in the effort to change your life fundamentally.

MARCH 2011

This morning, your ex girlfriend says she's walking with you to work.

"I need tissues," she says. She lifts a drawing off the ground and looks at it. "This is scary."

"You need tissues," you say.

"I need to keep some in my purse because of Babe."

Babe is her dad's toothless dog.

She's allergic.

"How is Babe," you say. "He was a good friend."

"He's good," she says. "His ear still smells like the inside of a cowboy boot."

"Did he lose any more teeth."

"Yeah like, all of them are basically gone," she says. "Are there any good sales on tissue then."

"Sales on tissues," you say. "I don't know." Running your tongue all over the inside of your mouth. "If you wait until we get to the store and then ask me though, I have to find out for you. Just wait until I clock in and then ask me. You can even try to get me fired if I refuse. We can make a big scene in the store and then get thrown out and come back here and go back to sleep and feel bad for ourselves."

"I want to drink something blue," she says, looking at the sock that's partially hanging off her foot.

You find yourself staring at her sock, then at one corner of the room where there's an old aluminum can that contains a large amount of fingernail rippings (and boogers) from just pacing around at night.

Probably going to throw it out soon—you think. Who knows.

"I'm going to take a shower," you say.

While you're showering, your ex girlfriend brings you a cup of coffee leftover in the fridge, mixed with hot chocolate mix.

You thank her.

She watches you shower for a little bit then leaves.

Your arm still hurts from trying to hold onto a heavy box while standing on a ladder last week.

It fucked up some forearm muscles.

Fingers are hard to control.

And you laugh about it, trying to hold the cup.

Thinking thoughts about suicide, but not in a desperate/dramatic way, more so like the way in which someone might consider joining the Army as an option for the future.

Halfway through the coffee, you pee in the shower.

The pee burns and smells bad.

You're staring at the peeling paint where the ceiling meets the showertile, and the black mold behind it.

Thinking about how when people say, "It could be worse"—that suggests it could be better too, and deciding to only think of it one way or another is to just make shit worse.

What you really want is to never be stupid enough to have feelings at all.

To be steady and unfeeling.

After the shower, you and your ex girlfriend sit on the Kiiiddzzz bed, putting on socks and shoes.

"What's Kiiiddzzzz," she says, touching one of the places where "Kiiidddzzzz" is printed on the bed.

"Kiiidddzz is who I am, basically. It's what I'm about. It's a lifestyle."

She sniffs like she's going to sneeze, then doesn't. "This bed is a fucking joke," she says. "It's like, for a baby. An actual newborn baby, I think. I'm not even joking."

"I'm not saying you're wrong," you say, looking at your blistered feet.

There's a nickel-sized blood blister on your little toe.

Filled with reddish-maroon liquid.

You hold out your bare foot to her.

"This is, somewhere on the bed family-tree between the ground and a real bed," she says.

"Look at the blister on my little toe, it's huge."

She holds her hair back and looks at the blister. "Oh shit," she says. "It looks like a little cranberry. Don't you have to pop it. Can I do it."

"No, the blood-ones you let heal," you say. "Then you can cut them off after they dry. Otherwise the blood can get infected if you do it while it's still juicy."

"Think you're wrong," she says, and stands up to button her coat. "You have to cut it to get the juice out."

You lift your foot a little higher and move the blistered toe back and forth. "Have a taste. Bite my little cranberry, eh."

She fakes like she's going to bite your blister.

A moment of intense fear happens inside you.

You say, "For some reason I've been fixated lately on imagining a metal grater of some kind going over my toenails, like backwards."

"Are all the lights off," she says.

"Yeah."

You leave the apartment together.

Going down the stairs she says, "Hey is your friend going to be there today, can I meet him."

"Theodore?"

"Yeah."

"I don't think he works Thursdays."

"Shit," she says.

Stepping outside, you find yourself thinking—They're all over my face.

Unsure of what.

*

On the walk to the store the sidewalks are still a little icy from an unseasonable snowstorm.

You and your ex girlfriend walk just off the sidewalk on the dirt.

She's a few feet behind you at all points except for crosswalks, where you watch opposite sides of traffic go opposite ways.

Talking about how when her mom still lived with them a long time ago, the mom always walked around naked and she had a huge bush between her legs.

"Like, it's just full in the front when she's wearing underwear too, and like, coming out the sides," your ex girlfriend says. "Like a diaper. Like imagine a chicken-legged woman with no ass and just these old, saggy-ass underwear on. With a giant bush in the front holding the underwear up."

"Shit," you say. "I just imagined it and it made me dizzy."

The only things you know about your ex girlfriend's mom is what your ex girlfriend told you—that the mom made your ex girlfriend and her sister run around outside with garbage bags taped to them to lose weight when they were really young, and made them dress up and participate in beauty pageants, and that she also instilled in them (at a young age) the fear of getting raped by their dad, because when the mom was younger, she got kidnapped and gangraped in Mexico.

That's all you've been told.

That and now the huge bush thing.

"Yeah a huge bush," she says, catching up behind you. "She had really nice boobs though, I'll give her that. She'd always call me into the bathroom to talk while she was in the bath and her boobs still looked really good. Why don't you want to walk with me. Are you thinking about my mom's boobs."

You don't say anything.

You've been just not answering people sometimes now.

This is becoming normal—you think. The highest freedom. To not say anything. To let it pass.

She says, "Why are you walking that fast, are you trying to ditch me."

"I'm just walking normal. It's how I always walk."

"I want to hold hands though," she says.

"I don't want to hold hands."

What you want is to walk into a giant bush of pubic hair and never return, to be taken in.

By the front entrance of the store, a homeless woman in a wheelchair asks for money.

She has a sweatshirt on with a sparkly American flag on the front and she's wearing post-eyesurgery sunglasses.

There's a golden retriever laying by her feet, smelling garbagey.

You give the woman a dollar.

"Two'd be better," she says, still holding out her hand, looking up with her post-eyesurgery sunglasses.

"No problem," you say, and give her another dollar. "Is two good. I have three more dollars but I was going to use them on my lunchbreak."

"No, two's good," she says, putting the money into a fannypack. "Thanks."

"You sure?"

"Yeah honey, thanks."

"Alright have a nice day," you say, noticing yourself as an ugly face on her sunglasses.

She wheels herself towards the bus stop.

The golden retriever follows.

Inside the store, a couple of the other backroom employees are up front.

Sour Cream is there.

He says, "Hey hey, what's going on what's going on"—typing things into his laser gun.

You don't say anything and neither does your ex girlfriend and everyone just stands there like assholes.

The store is loud.

A lot of people are shopping.

It creates a single sound.

Fluid leaks from your ear and you're dizzy.

Goddamnit—you think.

Another employee walks up, dropping off his keys at the front.

He has an earpiece walkie talkie on.

He works in electronics.

"Fucking done," he says, taking out the earpiece. He nods upward to your ex girlfriend then looks at you. He points at you, narrowing his eyes. "Oh hey," he says, "Did you know Timothy—we were all talking about him before—backroom guy, started here in the summer same time as you?"

"No, I didn't know Timothy," you say.

"Oh," he says, pushing up his glasses. "The guy who had all the seizures."

Sour Cream laughs twice in a high pitch and says, "Oh yeah, that guy. We found him having a seizure in the electronics stockroom once, right. That bald-ass white dude."

"Yeah," says the electronics employee, gesturing, "Then he got moved to the overnight shift. Well, he died today."

No one says anything.

You think about the punch combination George Foreman landed on Michael Moorer to become the oldest heavyweight champion in boxing history.

Two punches in close succession.

Left right.

The electronics employee says, "Yeah he had another seizure and swallowed his tongue, so—" he looks at the earpiece in his hand, folding his lips inward a little.

You find yourself folding your lips inward too.

Seems like what you're supposed to be doing.

No one says anything.

Hearts beat.

Blood does whatever it does.

Sour Cream says, "Shit," to himself—typing in more numbers on the laser gun, beeping sounds. "Wait, he died here you mean? Like, in the store."

The electronics employee looks up, his lips still folded inward. He raises his eyebrows and says, "What—no, somewhere else. Not in this store."

Your ex girlfriend says, "Alright guys. I'm going to get some Kleenex then."

You look at her and say, "Ok, go all the way down that side of the store, and they'll be on your left, towards the corner."

"Thanks," she says.

"Yeah."

She makes a very subtle motion forward with her face as if to kiss you and it's almost undetectable but you see it and counter by moving backwards, keeping the same distance the whole time.

"You lose," you say.

She looks at you like she's telling herself something.

Then she walks away.

Sour Cream watches her. He says, "Man she's fucking pretty, jo. You're lucky. I bet her pussy smell good as hell."

And you find yourself nodding, but also silently terrified you won't be able to resist the urge to try swallowing your own tongue throughout work.

*

After punching in, you walk back to the stockroom.

You pass by the section of the store where there's romance novels and magazines.

There's one called "The Rebel."

You stop and look at it.

On the front cover, there's a guy wearing a tanktop and sunglasses.

He's sitting on a ledge with his elbow on his knee.

The blurb at the bottom refers to the male character in the novel as '...scrumptious....'

Walking to the stockroom, you just want everything to be scrumptious from now on.

You don't want to be brave, honorable, reliable, important, significant, likable, trustworthy, confident, or anything other than scrumptious.

*

In the stockroom, someone comes out of an aisle, rolling a garbage can in each hand.

"N'Hey man, hm, what's up," he says, monotone.

"Hey Theodore," you say.

Theodore is the person who walks around the actual store area mopping things and cleaning things.

He pushes a large device that holds a lot of cleaning products and towels.

Theodore always has pink eye.

He's short and on the back of his head there is a large growth.

It's like a really big mole—flesh-colored and hairless.

The size of half a plum maybe.

You've wanted to bite it for so long.

Just once, to test the consistency.

Theodore.

He adds an "n" or "m" sound to a lot of words.

It makes everything he says hum.

"N'I got really sad last night, hm," he says.

"What happened man."

"N'I was watching my singing show'm, with my mom, hm. M'There was this freaking four year old girl, hm, and she lost. Yeah me and my mom, uhh, really liked her."

He's been telling you about this competitive singing show he watches every week with his mom.

"M'It was just so bad because, m'because everyone got sad for the four year old, and she could sing," he says. "She had talent up the wazoo, hmm."

You imagine Theodore playing an instrument called the "wazoo."

The instrument is like, a box with a long bagpipe-like mouthpiece and a crank you turn.

"M'She could sing so good, and only four freakin years old, hm," Theodore says, throwing his hand up into the air a little. "But she still lost. And my mom n'was sad too when we were watching it, hm. So bad."

"I mean, she probably still makes money off singing though," you say. "Like people will still give her money to sing. And the show was probably a nice experience for her."

Theodore makes the "ch" sound, stares for a little bit.

He says, "N'I found a whole boatload of flies in a lightbulb by the trash compactor today. N'It was filled with flies, hm."

"Were there flies up the wazoo."

He rolls his eyes, sighing dramatically and making the "ch" sound.

He says, "N'Yeah up the wazoo. Those hundred watt bulbs, hm, can hold n'a lot of flies, boy. Jeez, hm."

"Yeah."

"Ok. M'See you later man," he says.

"Bye, Theodore."

He waves goodbye in a way that looks more like he's trying to shake something off his hand that's biting him.

He rolls the garbage cans away.

*

Later on you decide to request a day off.

Not for any reason other than being able to know that that day will be off, no matter what.

To request a day off, you have to use the computer in the break-room.

It's a major move because it entails walking past the roomful of people to silently declare a need to use the computer.

It's like, who the fuck are you to use the computer.

Are you like, some important person who just needs to use the computer that other people might need to use.

What if a woman is waiting to use the computer to request a day off to go to the doctor and find out if her son has terminal cancer.

What if someone is waiting to request a day off to propose marriage.

What if someone is waiting to use the computer to request a day off so he or she can bring a gun dowtown and shoot people.

Things like that.

You pull the chair closer, sitting down at the computer.

The chair makes a loud sound sliding across the tile.

It embarrasses you.

Someone has left an email account open on the computer.

You pick a random email address from their inbox and email this message: "Alright—the gun is in locker F8 at the gym. You know what to do. No way out now."

You close out the email account and fill out the day off request form.

The form seems very difficult.

No focus, it melts together into a grid, or some horrible graph.

A grid-graph.

A horrible looking grid-graph.

You try to read.

Afraid the whole time.

Something could easily go wrong.

A spelling error.

A neglected box.

A computer virus.

A bomb.

A grid-graph.

A stroke.

A seizure.

Organ failure.

You imagine yourself at an expensive restaurant, saying, "One of each please" to an elegantly dressed waiter after the waiter recites the above list.

The day off form is right in front of your face.

You try to focus.

What if you don't fill out the form correctly.

You'd think you had, and then not come to work, then get fired, then not have money, then get discouraged and die.

It'd be the exact same thing as right now except you'd have a better reason to get discouraged and die.

Jesus, Mary, and Joseph.

You fill out the form slowly.

The first couple parts are easy.

Sometimes to refocus, you take a very deep breath and hold it in then blow it out.

Behind you, someone in the breakroom helloes another person.

Which begins a conversation.

One says, "Ey girl, is they a such thing as a baby rock. Lawanda said they was but she always lying."

The other says, "I'on't know. Fuck I know about rocks."

"Shee-yid," you say.

People laugh.

Staring at the computer screen, you repeatedly think—"I'on't know."

Feeling distracted.

You see yourself staggering into a hospital emergency room and then collapsing into a nurse's arms—and when he or she says, "What happened, sir" you weakly whisper back, "I've, been, distracted" and grip the nurse's shirt with a bloody hand.

The last part of the form involves clicking on a series of boxes on the screen that say, "Completed."

Leaving the breakroom, you project a feeling of relatively-high enjoyment knowing that once back at your apartment tonight, you'll be able to snip open the blisters on your feet and hands with nail-clippers—then drain the blisters and lie down—all without having to worry about contact from anyone.

In total control of your own quarantine.

Rewarding yourself for earning enough money to stay alive.

Reward through quarantine.

Snipping blisters.

The apartment is a waiting room.

It's nice.

You rent it.

Nurse—I've been—distracted.

Covered in blood.

I'on't know.

Outside the breakroom by the customer bathrooms, you openly reach into your pants to adjust your dick before going back to work so that it won't bother you when climbing ladders and bending down and whatnot.

A co-worker comes out the women's bathroom, tucking in her shirt.

You nod upward to each other, once.

She says, "Hey sweetie, you know if the Bulls won today?"

You scratch the back of your head and say, "No, I heard they all died in a plane crash on the way to whatever city they were going to play in."

She leans back to get the back part of her shirt tucked in and her bellybutton is visible in front as a wide impression behind her red shirt.

Probably could fit three fingers inside her bellybutton—you think.

"Shit," she says. "All of them died, huh. All of them. Sheesh that's awful."

"Yeah, even the pilot and all their pets too because I heard they brought their pets with them in the cargo area of the plane, you know, for luck."

"Goddamn," she says. "Un-believable."

"Yeah it's sad."

Then you both take turns asking each other what time your respective shifts will be done, to signal you'd both like to end the conversation.

*

Sometimes going out into the store is unavoidable.

You try to stay in the stockrooms—to avoid customers—but not all the stockrooms are connected.

Sometimes you have to leave them.

And sometimes you meet a man in corduroy pants who wants a new vacuum.

"Excuse me," he says. "I have a question. I'd like to see if you have this vacuum. It's this one over here."

He's about your age.

His face is cleanly shaven and he has a nice haircut and all the right buttons are buttoned on his shirt.

He's wearing a collared shirt tucked into corduroy pants, nice shoes, a tie and a belt.

You're amazed.

You follow him to the back wall where he points to a display model of the vacuum he wants.

You scan the upc code.

"Uh uh," you say, checking the screen. "We don't have any more of those."

And it's true.

There aren't any.

Sometimes you just answer no even if that's not true.

You'll type in a few buttons and say, "Uh, looks like no. We don't have any more. I'm sorry."

The man looks at the vacuum again, not saying anything.

"No more," you say again, in a friendly but firmly-settled way.

"Not at all huh? Darn," he says, making a playful face of disappointment.

"No more of those, sorry," you say, making a similar face.

Even though it's not your fault and you're not sorry.

Part of your pay comes from apologizing.

You entertain a violent fantasy of you and the man together in a bathroom, where you take stabs at his head with a cheap knife, and the blade is so cheap it keeps skipping off his skull, but still cuts deep.

He's still looking at the vacuum.

He says, "Alright well, I might just come in tomorrow or later this week to see if it's come in yet. I live nearby." He puts up both his hands with his fingers and thumbs out—"It's, sooo great you guys opened this place. Really great for the neighborhood."

You don't tell him it wasn't you who opened the store, that some other people did, the owners.

And you don't tell him that the neighborhood is good for the store, otherwise the owners wouldn't have opened it.

Because his eyebrows are perfect shapes—you think. Because he's friendly, and really understanding. Because he handled disappointment well. Not getting a new vacuum might cripple someone else. Send them into a crippling vertigo of despair. Not him though. His corduroy pants shield him from the crippling vertigo of despair.

"I really wanted this vacuum," he says, "so, I will, be back here for sure."

He smiles by flexing his bottom lip, tapping his fingers on the carthandle.

"You wanted this vacuum, right here," you say, pointing at the model.

"That one," he says.

You check the upc code and the model again, acting like you're using your thumb to closely read the upc.

"This one right here," you say.

He clicks his tongue. "That one."

You say, "Looks like a pretty good one. Like just, a good overall vacuum. I don't know that much about it, but I mean."

He starts biting the nail on his thumb. "Yeah," he says. "I've heard it's really good. The commercials are pretty impressive."

"Looks like it could do a good job," you say. "At least, that's what I'm thinking."

"No, yeah, the guy who invented it is supposed to be like, this genius."

"Uh oh."

"Yeah supposedly," he says, opening his eyes wide then returning them to normal wideness.

"Well he must be a genius to have invented such a great vacuum," you say, raking your front teeth over the hair directly below your bottom lip. "Don't you think."

"Yeah, of course," he says, "I mean my condo is screaming for this little number."

"What little number," you say.

"The vacuum," he says.

"Oh nice. Did your last vacuum stop working. What happened."

"No," he says, "Just didn't have the type of power I need right now in a vacuum, specifically. Plus it was clunky and loud."

You sneeze.

You say, "And then you came here and we didn't have the one you wanted—man."

"Yeah," he says.

"Man, sorry," you say. "I wish—wait"—you pause and type some numbers into the laser gun again— "Ah, nope. Thought I might've typed in the wrong number before."

You imagine the man returning tomorrow in a slightly different combination of the same clothes he's in now—picking up the newly stocked vacuum and buying it—driving it home in the passenger side seat of his car, seatbelt across its box—bringing it into his house—opening the box—vacuuming with a slight smile on his face—vacuuming thoroughly, without stopping for a long time.

But secretly, he's never happy with any vacuum.

He's never, fucking, happy.

So he blames the vacuum.

Always looking for a different kind, a kind that will work like he wants.

"Alrighty, no problem," he says, walking away.

It's unclear how much time has passed in silence.

You look at the display model of the vacuum the man wanted.

A salesfloor employee told you a while ago that customers can't buy the models because the models aren't functional.

Looking at the nonfunctioning model, you imagine yourself without any inside parts—like organs or veins or genitals.

Then you realize you can only imagine that idea by using all your inside parts.

It's fucking weird.

You're fake.

*

On your lunch break you're eating an apple, sitting at a table with an uncomfortable amount of other people at it.

There's a lower level manager, a girl sitting next to you, a bald man with a beard, and some other people.

The girl next to you is reading a magazine for women that talks about exercising, and has sexual quizzes, and advertisements, and other things.

"'Right before his very thighs,'" you say, reading off the magazine. "'How to find secret pleasure spots on him, pg. 43.'"

The girl opens her eyes wide and starts turning pages. "Ooh, should we read 'The top five signs he's an alpha male.'"

"Yeah, top five signs," you say.

The lower level manager is eating food from the food area at the store.

It's a pizza made small so as to be for one person.

A miniature pizza.

He picks up a piece of the miniature pizza and bites it.

Then he takes a napkin from the stack in front of him and wipes his fingers and goatee.

"Wow this is the first time I've bought a pizza here that actually had sauce on it," he says, to no one. Then he addresses the entire table, and says, "Alright so, if you absolutely had to, would you be able to eat another human."

The bald man with a beard is also eating a miniature pizza and there's sauce on his moustache.

When he hears the question, he lowers his eyebrows and nods.

"Oh hell yeah I would," he says. "Hell yeah. No question. Don't be stupid. But it's like, what part would you eat though. Like in what order. I think the ass probably has the most meat. The ass is just all meat, man."

The lower level manager says, "The legs seem appealing to me for some reason, I don't know. It's weird."

You straighten up in your seat, elbows on the table. "Albert Fish said ass meat was his favorite. He wrote letters to his friend about it."

The girl reading the magazine says, "Ass meat"— still turning pages looking for an article.

The bald bearded guy says, "Well, are we talking about kids or what are we talking about."

The girl reading the magazine says, "We're talking about ass meat."

Chavon is sitting at the end of the table.

She's sharing a set of in-ear headphones with the guy next to her, and he's got his head down bobbing to the music.

Chavon says, "Me, I'm straight eating fingers right away."

Then she makes—what you decide to be—a "gobbling motion" with her hands and mouth, and the headphone falls out of her ear.

You laugh.

Chavon laughs.

She points at you and says, "Texas knows it. Look at'yo special ass. This motherfucker special."

The lower level manager delicately bites a portion of his miniature pizza and repeats his napkin wiping routine.

He says, "Yeah I'd do like, the calf muscles first, I think. Get a good meal out of that first."

You think about biting a calf muscle as hard as you can.

Getting on hands and knees and crawling out into the store,

finding someone who's looking at a product on the shelves, then biting their calf muscle as hard as you can, shaking your head a little to make it rip.

Stomach swollen with blood and muscle.

The girl next to you puts the magazine on the table.

"Here it is— top five signs. Are you ready. Or no, let's take this quiz instead. It says, 'Beach Quiz.'"

"Beach quiz beach quiz," you say in an excited voice, slapping your thighs.

The other people at the table start talking about whether or not the show on the breakroom tv has vampires in it and the girl reads you the quiz.

You watch her face as she reads the quiz.

She says, "Ok, question one—" then looks somewhere else on the page, "Oh wait. Oh this article's called 'The naughtiest thing you've ever done.' Should we read that instead."

"What did the person do," you say. "If it's too naughty, don't tell me."

She scans the article, pushing her glasses back against her face.

"Oh god," she says, "This is retarded. It says, 'I stole my roommate's man in college.'"

"My roommate's man," you say.

"Yeah," she says. "It says, 'I stole my roommate's man, for a dormroom fling.'"

You say, "Wait, what happened—there was a dormroom fling you say."

She reads from the magazine. "'We cut class, but he still gets an A+ in my opinion.'"

"It'd be funny if someone confessed to a brutal hit and run accident, in vivid detail," you say. "Like if that was the naughty thing the person did I mean."

The bald bearded man says, "Hah, it's like, 'When I drove away, I could see him clutching a bloody crack on the top of his skull, crawling in the street.'"

The lower level manager is staring at the tv, holding a miniature piece of pizza up to his face.

He says, "'Broken glass clung to his face and he crawled blindly in the street over his own blood.'"

No one says anything for a little bit.

"That's not funny," says the girl reading the magazine, turning to another page.

A skinny guy with razor scars all over his arms is typing something into his phone. "It's funny, sweetie," he says, snapping a baby carrot with his front teeth.

You hold out your apple to the girl with the magazine.

"Do you want some of this apple. It's great."

She takes the apple and bites it.

She hands it back, not looking up from the magazine.

You watch her wet mouth chew.

This is beautiful—you think. This is 100%. This is freedom.

The way she's bending the magazine, it looks to you like one of the articles on the front cover says, "College Hernia Blood!? Hwqja!"

Sounds like a good article—you think, feeling the impossibility of knowing where to look.

That's a recurring feeling for you: Where should I be looking.

On the back cover of the magazine there's an advertisement.

You read it out loud. "Max-out your volume, with Aloe and Avocado."

The girl turns a page and says, "Max-out, bitch."

Chavon says, "We live maxed-out."

The guy sharing headphones with her rhymes: "Maxed-out/fact is, crack's clout/and we smash clowns/stash cash-mounds in mattresses here in Uptown."

Chavon says, "Nice."

The lower level manager sets down a piece of his miniature pizza and says, "Hey did you staple the receipt to the magazine cover."

The girl looks up from her magazine. "What."

She flips her hair to the side.

Anger.

You feel in love, for however long a half-second is.

Knowing a half-second is long enough to be in love.

The manager wipes some grease off his goatee.

"You're supposed to staple the receipt to the cover so we know you didn't just take it," he says. "Otherwise how do we know."

The girl immediately gets loud. "What. I'm not going to ruin the magazine I just bought. I paid for it earlier. Check the fucking security footage if you need to. God."

You hit the table with your fist and say, "Check the footage"—in a way meant to encourage animosity between them.

The bald bearded guy says, "Check the footage."

"I'm just saying, that's policy," says the lower level manager. He wipes his fingers on a napkin. "You're supposed to do that."

You look at her and say, "You're supposed to do that."

"Ok fine, now I know," she says, flipping her hair to the side and looking at the magazine again. "Fuck. I'm not going to steal a fucking magazine this stupid. God."

The lower level manager looks at his miniature pizza, then you.

He says, "Hey, before I forget, can you certify the new stockroom trainee before you go home today."

"Yeah, I'd love to—absolutely," you say, hitting the table with your hand again.

"Alright, thank you sir," he says. "It's some guy with freckles."

"Guy with freckles?" you say, pointing at the lower level manager.

He looks at you, a little confused. "Yeah."

You hit the table with your hand and say, "Ok great, thanks."

APRIL 2011

This morning it takes a lot of effort to stay awake after waking up—which is becoming normal.

It's around seven a.m.

You stay in bed, going in and out of sleep, body hurting.

People make noise at the bus stop outside.

People are always outside.

Always around.

You half-dream/half-imagine a large pile of shit you keep putting your head in then taking back out.

When you pull your head out of the shit, terrible strings of pulp are wrapped around your head and face.

But then, you have regular air.

And after one breath, you put your head back into the shit.

And do it slow enough to really feel it.

Because it could never be different—you think.

And your complaints diffuse to the renewed beginning of traffic sounds, ambulance sounds, airplane sounds, people sounds, and television sounds from another apartment.

Trying to wake up.

Somebody walks past your window, on Clark Street.

He screams/sings, "Everyone gonna *die*, gonna *die*, gonna *die*"—sustaining every third "die."

His singing voice is a combination of singing/yelling/laughing, and he walks down the block gone.

Your neighbor.

Three million others too, surrounding.

You quietly sing, "Everyone gonna die, gonna die, gonna die."

It's a good song.

Yes.

A fine song, for the beginning of another fine day.

Yesterday at work one of the managers was helping you throw out garbage and she said, "Guess what, I think I met my future husband last night, on a date."

She had her front teeth over her bottom lip, excited.

You said, "You met your husband from the future?"

Then you thought about how his time travelling would change your life, and how you'd never even notice, because this thought would be one of its results.

Fuck!

"We went out last night," she said. Then she swung a bag of garbage into the compactor, leaning forward to avoid getting garbage juice on her shirt. She checked her breasts and said, "He's from South Carolina. He's an engineer and he's six foot one"—opening her eyes wide then returning them to normal wideness.

You said, "So that's already three facts you know about him. That's good."

In your Kiiidddzzzz bed, you think about her breasts shaking as she swung bags of garbage into the compactor.

And your dick gets very hard but you're too tired to touch it—trying to wake up.

The room is lighter.

Same color as always.

You let your dick be hard, lying on your back on your sweet fucking Kiiidddzzzzz bed.

The front door to the apartment building slams shut, and then footsteps come up the stairway.

Someone knocks at your apartment door.

More knocking.

Key-sounds.

The door opens and someone walks into your apartment.

You hear, "Hallo? Hallo?" as someone stomps in.

There's a knock at your bedroom door.

"Hallo? Hallo?"

The door opens.

It's the "Building Manager."

He puts his head into the room from behind the door.

The Building Manager is an old Serbian man the landlord exploits for manual labor.

He's old and has bad knees and barely ever has the tools he needs.

You're lying in bed.

Eyes half-closed.

Dick hard.

Looking at an old Serbian man sticking his head sideways into the room.

"Hallo? Hallo?" he says. "Hallo? You awake? Hallo hallo. I come to fix roof. There is problem with roof. I go up now, ok? Hallo? You awake buddy, hallo. Wass wrong? You alive buddy, hallo."

You say, "There's a new leak in the hallway. I think it's because someone just painted over the leak last time."

"Yes ok. I go see. Ok? Tank you buddy."

You lie in bed letting your dick get soft while the old Serbian man looks at the same leaking spot in the hallway ceiling he's seen many times now.

Then he leaves the apartment.

Thirty seconds later, he's walking around on the roof.

It's very loud.

You continue to fall in and out of sleep, halfway worried about the old Serbian man falling through the roof, crushing you—snapping your hard dick at a horrible angle.

How you'd lie there half-asleep looking at your angled dick, broken like a dandelion stem.

You get out of bed.

You see a bright yellow light in your eyes and put your hand against the wall so you don't fall.

Die. Die. Die.

In the bathroom, you put your head beneath the showerhead, standing outside the shower.

The water is very hot and you have your finger in your left ear to keep water out.

You mouth, "In Chi-town, you in *my* town—it's kill or die motherfucker, kill or die."

You turn off the shower and take your finger out of your ear.

Liquid comes out.

You soak it out with a twisted piece of toilet paper.

The toilet paper is brown and red when you take it out.

This is painful—you think. But I deserve this.

And your self-esteem today is shaky.

Shaky but stabilizing into something even lower and unshakable.

*

After punching in at work, you walk through the store to the stock-room.

Passing the pharmacy area, there's a group of gradeschool aged kids standing there, kicking each other.

One of the kids holds out his hand to you and says, "Ey, let me get it right here, my nigga."

You high-five, shake, and snap with his hand.

The group of gradeschool kids yells and laughs.

Without turning around, you flex both arms, walking towards the stockroom.

*

Theodore is on break the same time as you.

He's sitting next to you, wearing a Styrofoam visor with a dolphin on it, from the John G. Shedd Aquarium.

He's using a fork to cut a still mostly frozen microwaveable dinner.

The food breaks with a brittle cracking sound.

"Theodore, how are you," you say.

He says, "N'Hey. What's up man, hm."

He tells you about how a few weeks ago they had to have a plumber come out to fix all the clogs in the toilets and when they fixed the clogs they found a bunch of hypodermic needles people had flushed in the customer bathrooms.

"I like your dolphin visor, man," you say.

"M'Yeah," he says. "N'I saw the freakin dolphin show already, hm. Wow. N'Yeah I saw the dolphin show with my mom and the dolphins were absolutely wonderful, hm."

His right leg is rapidly going up and down, on toe-point.

He scrapes icy pieces of food with the fork.

You say, "You liked the dolphin show."

"N'Yeah," he says. "To be cuppletely honest though, N'I went with my mom to the dolphin show and I think, hm, my mom is pretty, hm."

Someone turns up the volume on the breakroom television.

The television is so loud the sound distorts.

An audience is laughing.

It hurts your infected ear.

Theodore says, "N'Yeah when I was little hm, and I'd get a loose tooth, n'my mom would help me take it out. N'I'd be in bed and she'd get on top of me and hold me down and m'have some freakin tissue paper in her fingers, hm, to be able to hold the tooth good and pull hard enough, hm. N'That's how she helped me get my baby teeth out, hm. N'Yeah sometimes when she was pulling, m'there was—there was," he pauses, then says, "pain" loudly.

He maintains the same tone as his talking, just louder.

The suddenness makes your heart beat faster a few times, and you narrowly avoid shitting your pants.

"N'And then but that's how she pulled all the baby teeth out, oh man!" he says. "N'Yeah. One of the times she was only wearing a freakin t-shirt, hm. N'And she smelled like the shower. M'And she was on my pee pee and but so until it got hard." He yells, "Got big."

The door to the breakroom opens.

One of the higher-up managers puts her head inside the breakroom doorway.

She has a store phone with the mouthpiece against her chest.

"Theo, be quiet hun," she says. "And when you're done with lunch hun, do the garbage in the women's bathroom."

"M'uh oh," he says.

"It's not bad, the garbage is just full," she says, smiling and raising her eyebrows. "No poop. I'm going to help though, k?"

Theodore makes the "ch" sound.

Then he says, "N'Yeah alright."

The manager puts the phone back to her mouth, continuing a conversation as she goes back out the doorway.

Theodore continues talking to you because you're still looking at him.

"N'My pee pee got hard sometimes when my mom was n'on top of me," he says. "I think she's really pretty to be cuppletely honest, hm."

"Cool," you say.

He breaks the frozen food into more of a consistent form, scratching his head behind the Styrofoam dolphin visor.

You look at the bald growth on the back of his head.

Just one bite.

Theodore says, "N'Yeah but I got some quarters and a piece of candy for every tooth. The next day, hm. N'I always got those presents."

He fixes his Styrofoam dolphin visor, and eats a bite of the frozen dinner.

"That's pretty good for one tooth," you say.

He nods his head, looking at his food. "N'Yeah."

"So the dolphin show was good. Should I see the dolphin show then. You liked it."

"N'Yeah the dolphin show was real great and the dolphins jumped high," he says, scraping the frozen food. "It was m'my favorite of all! Wow!"

You both laugh.

For the remainder of break, you watch a gameshow where they give you an answer, and you have to provide the question that leads to it.

Like if the answer given is: "The guy sitting next to you wearing a Styrofoam dolphin visor"—you'd say, "Who is Theodore."

Same thing as the other way around.

Each new question, Theodore rises a little out of his chair and says, "Hm hm"— like he's about to answer—but then never does.

You keep answering, "Airplane" for every question.

Theodore laughs at first.

Then he just stares at the gameshow eating his slush.

You look at the bald growth on his head and stand up to go back to work.

It's very hard to balance.

The breakroom is so bright.

*

An hour before your shift is over, you're breaking down boxes by the compactor.

By the compactor, there's the garbage lift.

The lift is a sheetmetal platform that rises up to the garbage compactor in the wall.

Theodore is beneath the garbage lift, sweeping up Styrofoam.

It's his job to raise the lift and sweep beneath it every night.

He's slightly bent over beneath the platform talking to you, his mouth hidden by one of the risers.

It's just eyes and hair as he's talking.

He says, "N'uh wow, this is like uh, Jacques Cousteau's untold adventure'm."

You say, "Yeah. Nice."

He says, "N'I bought a dvd of some of my favorite classic cartoons yesterday because I got my paycheck n'and the dvd was on freakin clearance, hm. Wow."

"Nice," you say.

"N'yeah it has all the good ones on it and I got it for, hm, four dollars m'so I can still buy my mom some slippers for Easter. Hm."

"Awesome."

"N'yeah the dvd has Garfield on it, hm. It was"—he stops, and sneezes a violent sneeze. A loop of clear snot hangs off his nose. "N'I like Garfield except for the ones with that pesky little runt Nermal. N'I really hate Nermal, hm."

"I hate Nermal too," you say, staring at the loop of snot on his nose. "He's really pesky."

"N'I hate Nermal so much," he says. He wipes his nose with the back of his wrist. "M'He's always messing around, hm."

You notice he's actually upset, and might cry.

"Fuck Nermal," you say. "He's nothing. He's nobody."

"N'yeah, I hate Nermal, hm."

"Me too," you say. "He's shit."

Theodore smiles, sweeping beneath the sheetmetal platform.

You consider crushing him.

Yeah.

Just grab the control and lower the lift.

Then when he tries to get out, kick him in the stomach or chest as hard as you can with your steel-toed boot—all the while still deftly handling the lift control.

You could do it.

Of course you could.

You wouldn't actually crush him though.

You'd make the sheet metal lift go as close to killing him as possible—just to trap him.

You'd be able to do that if you wanted.

Of course you would.

Because you're a competent, successful, and ambitious man, with a rich future.

Deserving of everything that happens, exactly as it happens.

MAY 2011

This morning, you go to Union Station with your ex girlfriend and drop her off at a train to her dad's house.

Inside Union Station there's a large vestibule area where homeless people sleep on rows of wooden benches, beneath a high dome-ceiling.

Where footsteps and voices echo at a sustained low pitch.

You sit on a ledge in the arrivals hallway, right past the vestibule area.

You watch passengers arrive, looking for repeats of people arriving, to see if your life is fake.

But there are no repeats.

Just more and more people arriving, walking through benches of the sleeping homeless.

Across the vestibule area there's a small arcade area.

You walk over and buy a drink from one of the vending machines.

The only other person in the arcade is an Amish man.

He walks around with his arms behind his back, looking at the videogames.

He stands by one of the machines watching the screen, where there are people murdering each other, and bombs going off.

He walks over to a game where the player has to sit in a plastic car.

You watch him sit in the car and press the brakes, press some buttons.

He stares at the desert scene on the screen as he turns the steeringwheel side to side really hard, many times.

It sounds like "gunk-gunk-gunk."

His face looks steady, or unsure, or something else.

Gunk-gunk-gunk.

Another man walks into the arcade area and starts playing a game with a plastic gun you aim at the screen and shoot at mutated people who have blood on their faces.

The Amish man gets out of the plastic car and watches, keeping his hands behind his back.

You feel upset.

But you can't tell if it's about the Amish man or yourself.

Then you realize you're upset about always feeling upset for other people, and for making-up reasons to be upset.

Mostly, it doesn't make sense.

The Amish man and you stand by the man playing the videogame and watch him shoot people on the screen.

And you try not to laugh, thinking about sitting in the videogame car with the Amish man, driving away together into the videogame desert.

*

When you get to work, the punch-in machine won't let you punch-in.

You try a few times then check the schedule.

It says, "Unavailable" over that day's box.

Today is the day you requested off a long time ago.

After a hot dog from the food area, you go for a walk north into Uptown.

It's warm out.

Twenty feet from a crosswalk, a little girl with beaded hair holds her hand up and says, "Reh light."

You stop mid-step and balance.

She seems excited.

She keeps it at red light for what seems to you like an unnecessary amount of time.

Then she puts her hand down and says, "Green light."

"Oh man, thanks," you say, and resume walking.

And it occurs to you that you'd probably experience a large amount of excitement and satisfaction from buying a flower of some kind and raising it from a seed—like if you really put in effort to take care of it as best you could.

It also occurs to you, you're worried that once dead you'll have to watch your life on an endless loop until memorized completely.

And part of the endless loop will be the part where you begin watching the loop.

Which then forms more loops, each one taking you with, never finishing.

An incomplete repetition that is never the same and always unfolds inside-out unendingly.

You're worried it's enough to consider that happening, to make it happen.

Goddamnit.

Behind a high school, you piss on the side of a dumpster.

The piss comes out itchy.

This is the part of the loop where you piss on a dumpster, and realize you're the only person you care about.

Staring at a mural made of broken tile, on the side of the high school.

The mural is four open-mouthed heads, floating, and above them these two cupped hands pour water down.

You shake your dick and tuck it back in.

You look at the mural again.

The mural looks different.

But it's not.

No.

It's still a pair of cupped hands dropping water down onto a bunch of floating heads, on the side of a high school.

What is different.

No.

Nothing is different.

You don't care.

Exiting the alley, you find a dead bird smashed into the ground, right by where the alley meets with the street.

You kick the dead bird and feathers come off.

A car drives by the alley, and the person in the passenger side seat yells, "Faggot."

What's most upsetting to you about people yelling shit as they drive by is not what they say, but the way it startles you and how you just have to stand there dazed until fully-recovered.

Admit it.

Admit it doesn't matter how many more days there are left, it matters how many seconds.

You stop at a franchise sandwich place and order food, sitting in a booth waiting for your order.

You stare at your folded hands, trying to remember something.

Unsure what.

Two guys in the next booth talk about whether or not it would be possible to kill a cat with a single punch.

"No man, telling you—I could do it," one says.

The other says, "You'd have to hit it just right to do it—sss—man, I don't know."

You hope to be invited into the conversation but you are resolved not to invite yourself.

*

Back at the apartment, you eat in your room.

Then you throw the balled-up wrapper against the wall as hard you can from a seated position.

You do push-ups.

JUNE 2011

On your last fifteen-minute break today you go out front of the store
and sit on a concrete ledge by the bus stop.

The stockroom is at least fifteen degrees warmer than the rest of
the store, and you've been sweating all day.

It's been really hot for a while but tonight it's supposed to cool
down again.

A man in some kind of plastic wheelchair device rolls himself up
to the bus stop.

He brakes near the ledge and starts talking to you.

You can't understand what he's saying.

It's like he can't think of words, or how to say them.

He's just sitting in an unstable wheelchair, mumbling.

You stand from the ledge to get closer.

There are bad dandruff things in his hair.

He keeps talking but you can't understand what he's saying.

Eventually, it's agreed that what he's asking is for you to go into
the store and buy him one gallon of milk and three bananas.

You just guessed.

You know that's not what he's saying, but every time you say,
"So, a gallon of milk and three bananas"—he nods his head yes.

His body odor smells like burnt motor-oil, and he holds out some
money to you with a shaking hand, fingernails cracked.

You spend the rest of break buying him a gallon of milk and three
bananas.

You bring him the gallon of milk and the three bananas and put
it all in his lap.

He mumbles something you can't understand.

"My break is over," you say. "I have to go back."

You return to work.

*

An hour later when you check for carts out front, the same man is still there.

He's on the ground now, gripping the plastic wheelchair device and trying to get back up into the seat.

The bananas and milk are on the sidewalk.

Two women at the bus stop make concerned looks and gestures, pointing.

They stand there watching.

You look at the man and say, "Hey man, do you need help."

He just keeps mumbling.

Keeps trying to stand but his legs look all numb and useless and his arms shake when he grips the armrests, trying to climb back in.

Keeps falling.

You grab him by the armpits and lift him.

It's difficult.

He's very heavy and the plastic wheelchair is unstable.

He's saying something to you the whole time you're lifting him, but you can't understand him.

His body odor is strong and you keep your face away from the bad dandruff things in his hair, afraid they'll get on your lips.

You lower the man back into his plastic wheelchair then wheel him over by the garbage cans where he's pointing and grunting.

You leave him there and walk back towards work feeling strangely bothered.

But this is freedom—you think.

The milk and the bananas are still on the ground.

You leave them there.

It's cooling down fast outside and there seems to be another sheen of light over the already existing light of the city.

When you try to focus on it you fail.

A planes flies past, nearing to land.

Fuck you—you think.

There are no carts out front.

You go back into the store and continue working.

*

When your shift is done, you exit through the front of the store.

The man in the plastic wheelchair is gone.
The milk and bananas are gone.
It's around one a.m.
You walk home.
The sidewalks are quiet.
Besides you, the only thing moving is wind.
Fuck you, wind—you think.
Then you think about how even if you walked all night, the edge of the city would still just be an unaccomplished distance.
Only the dark would eventually escape.
Only the dark, having shown itself, would then retire.
And you wish that same opportunity was yours.
That same chance.
Back inside your apartment, you kneel in the doorway to untie your boots.
Your hands smell like body odor from lifting the man up by the armpits.
You make guns with each hand then point them at the wall, doing gun-sounds with your mouth.
It's your twenty-eighth birthday.

CPSIA information can be obtained at www.ICGtesting.com
Printed in the USA
LVOW13s0828121113

360980LV00001B/26/P

9 781936 383764